THROUG

Suddenly, the universe around him went dark, as the stars sucked into a point behind his back, blurring and disappearing in red smears. The rest was an image constructed from nerve impulses that reached him an eternity after the event they recorded had ceased to exist. He was inside the hyperfold. Before his eyes all was double vision. He didn't know if he was losing consciousness or if it was only the familiar sense of time reversal inside the fold. Perhaps both.

Then Philip Holder slid into oblivion as his stolen craft accelerated with all the power it could muster. If he had calculated incorrectly, even by a fraction of a per cent, he would never wake up.

But if it worked, he would have embarked on the most awesome journey ever taken by man.

Bantam Books by Paul Preuss

THE GATES OF HEAVEN
RE-ENTRY

6

"Citizen Jerome?" the maitre d' inquired politely.

"That's right," Susan replied.

"Officer Claymore is waiting for you on the terrace. If you'll step this way . . ."

Susan trailed the obsequious helot through the crowded dining room. This Claymore must throw some weight, thought Susan, to rate an outside table at this hour, in this kind of weather.

The day was warm, so warm that the restaurant roof had been rolled back. Claymore's table was on the very edge of the deck, where one could look down the sheer sides of the ancient, weather-beaten soleri to the landscaped slopes of Mount Parnassus far below, and on out over San Francisco's endless blocks of slum shacks, a grayish-white vista relieved only by the huge stained oblong dome over Golden Gate Park. In the distance, the ocean and the bay glittered in the brown haze, and a few kilometers farther to the north, beyond the rusted broken teeth of the Bridge, the outline of the Tamalpais soleri was vaguely discernible in the murk.

"Here you are, Citizen," said the helot.

"Thank you," Susan said to the man. Most doctors would have insisted on the use of their title, thus humiliating the easily humiliated creature, but Susan was content to be called Citizen, and she insisted instead on treating helots as if they were human beings—though she doubted they noticed.

Claymore was standing. She extended a hand graciously. Susan shook it perfunctorily.

"You're much younger than I expected," Susan said bluntly.

Claymore smiled, showing perfectly even teeth in a heart-shaped face. Susan enviously noted that the government agent was wearing a fortune in genuine cotton and leather, all in the finest taste. The two women settled into their chairs, assisted by helots. The headwaiter presented Susan with a menu tab, then bowed and left. Rather obstinately, Susan said nothing, waiting for Claymore to start the conversation—after all, Claymore was filthy rich, one of *them*. Beautiful besides, the eyes especially, dark and liquid . . .

Susan blinked. "Pardon me for staring," she said. She'd spoken first after all. "I must seem terribly rude. . . ."

Claymore smiled again. "But you're not at all sure you approve of me, is that it?"

"Since you mention it." Susan felt inadequate to the demands of the interview, conscious of her own imitation silk suit, her rather thin, pale, unusually blonde looks.

"I have no intention of seducing you into liking me," Claymore said, with what sounded like genuine sympathy. "I asked to meet you here only because it is an exceptionally fine day, this is an exceptionally fine view, and this is my first visit to San Francisco. I admit to combining business with pleasure whenever possible."

"I can hardly argue with that," said Susan.

"Good. Why don't you order? And then we can talk."

Susan flicked off a number of items on the menu tab, sparing the government no expense. She knew the vegetables here were crisp and fresh and frightfully costly. A silent waiter appeared just as she held out the tab, taking it in a gloved hand and soundlessly disappearing.

"Will you join me?" Claymore asked, indicating the bottle of white burgundy cooling in the silver bucket beside her chair. Indeed Susan would. As they sipped, Claymore explained the purpose of her trip, concluding, "Naturally, we'd like to close the matter as soon as possible."

"I'm surprised there's any question in your mind," Susan replied. "The news people all seem satisfied it was an elaborate suicide."

"And you?"

"Phil behaved in a classically self-destructive manner for years, there's no doubt of that. Frankly, I got sick of wiping up his messes." Susan paused, looking at Claymore. For no reason she could put her finger on, she decided to trust the woman. "You know we were lovers? For awhile at least. I assume you know that."

"Yes."

"It was after his second wife was . . . died. I knew them both."

"We have the public facts, Susan," Claymore said gently. "By the way, my name is Angelica."

Oddly, the proffered intimacy seemed neither out of place nor premature. Susan accepted gratefully, looking into Claymore's remarkable eyes. "He was extraordinarily sensitive, so sensitive sometimes I actually thought he was reading people's minds. Reading my mind. He used to get upset when I'd say that, though." Susan paused, remembering. "I'd get a lecture on how all you had to do was watch people, their eyes, their reactions to other people—with that and a little data about their pasts, you could fill in the rest. Even the broad outlines of their future."

"That must have been useful in his profession."

"It wasn't just professional, Angelica. It was almost as if he couldn't help it."

"What happened between you?" Claymore asked softly. The warm breeze of the early June afternoon stirred her chestnut hair. Otherwise she did not move, fixing her gaze on Susan.

"I just got tired," Susan answered. "Tired of his drinking. Tired of his other women—his little girls. Tired of his *despair*. He seemed to think the past had condemned him. He talked about it all the time. His first wife. His son. His *second* wife. I tried to sympathize, but after a while . . . after I got tired of hearing him talk, nothing else seemed worth putting up with."

"So you broke off with him?"

Susan nodded. "Not that it did any good. He'd still collapse on my doorstep whenever he was in trouble." She sighed shortly, glaring around. "I hate these damn soleris sometimes, don't you? You can never get away from anybody."

"They were a good idea once, when they made a little more space. I'm afraid we've run out of that."

Susan dropped her gaze, ashamed. "Maybe I shouldn't complain." Her gaze flickered to the edge of the balcony. "After all, what if I weren't in the ninetieth percentile? I'd be living down there . . ."

Claymore looked at Susan sympathetically, encouraging her to go on. "Was there some particular time—some specific incident—that made you suspect Phil might have decided to kill himself?"

"Oh, that was always a possibility, right from the beginning." Susan stared at her. "It was kind of a bitter joke between us—he'd accuse me of putting up with him only because I'm a pathologist."

Claymore arched her eyebrows. "I don't . . ."

"Of waiting to get my hands on his corpse," Susan specified, embarrassed.

"Not exactly Attic wit," Claymore said coolly.

"He was usually drunk when he said it." She sighed. "After I stopped seeing him it got worse, if possible. For months. Worse and worse and worse. I was even considering . . ." She stopped, swallowing.

"Susan?" Claymore asked with concern.

Susan's eyes were closed, as if she were holding back tears. "Well, he was just getting so awful. I was getting so desperate. I . . . I almost called Security. Even though . . . you . . ."

"Even though you were afraid we'd 'burn him,' " Claymore finished for her.

"Oh, I know you don't do it unless they ask for it," Susan said bitterly. "But how do they *know* . . .?" Susan's eyes strayed.

Among the neighboring tables in the busy restaurant glided attentive helots, polite, competent, wholly devoid of pride. At some time in the past each of them had voluntarily sought brainburning, with its guarantee of government maintenance for the duration of one's natural life, its assurance of pleasant work, neither interesting nor overly strenuous, its promise of release from past associations, from squalor, from pain, from ambition.

"However, you decided against reporting Phil," Claymore prompted.

"He changed. It was about two years ago now, I guess. I only saw him a few times during that period. He seemed incredibly busy, driven almost. He made two trips outside the solar system, maybe three. And he stopped drinking, or at least, he stopped getting drunk. And I think I know why . . ." Susan stopped again, aware that what she was about to say would sound foolish.

"Please go on," said Claymore.

"Somehow he got hold of the idea he *could* go back to his past. That he could make it right."

"Go back? Time travel?" Claymore smiled.

Susan blushed. "It sounds crazy, doesn't it?"

"It does seem pretty far-fetched."

"Well, I don't believe it myself. But I think Phil did."

Susan looked seriously at Angelica Claymore. "He may be dead, but whatever he was doing out there that night, he wasn't just giving up." She paused. "Somehow it's important to me for you to know that."

Claymore said nothing.

If Susan could have read Claymore's mind—as Phil Holder might have, or as Claymore read Susan's—she would have been appalled by what she found there.

But Claymore weighed Susan's last words, and decided Susan was sincere when she said she didn't think time travel was a real possibility. Therefore Claymore decided to allow Susan to go on thinking.

"At last! Here's our food," said Claymore, as the helot brought a large silver tray. Claymore raised her wine glass in Susan's direction. "Doctor, to your health."

7

"By now Tanner knew that her daring experiments, using herself as subject, had been unequivocally successful. Over a ten-year period she had continuously plotted over two dozen functions of the body, on every level from cell membrane ion exchange to blood oxygen absorption, and at every level she found the same result: no change over time. She had gone far beyond the work of her predecessors. She had not only slowed the aging processes, she had stopped them in their tracks.

"There was one exception to the otherwise cheery picture: she was sterile. Her ovaries had not produced a viable gamete in a decade, and she knew they never would again. The primitive medical techniques of the period could not alleviate her resulting depression. She disappeared from public view, and never published a word of her findings.

"In retrospect, we know that it was sometime

during this period that Margaret Tanner relinquished the name she had been born with. Many years later and many light-years away from Earth we are able to resume the story of Clarissa Sirich, now living under the name Elizabeth Tanaka. . . ."

(from *Darwin: A Millennium of Conservation*)

Before Darwin's Star there was Bounty's Star. Before Darwin there was Bounty.

Before Bounty there was nothing but a barren rock circling WSC 1228, the one thousand, two hundred and twenty-eighth star identified by the old Project Cyclops' Whole Sky Catalogue as a single star of clement temperature with a high probability of possessing planets.

In and of itself the rock was ugly, but a couple of traits made it interesting to speculators in planetary real estate. Its mass was only a few thousandths of a percent less than Earth's, and though its sun was hotter, a G-0 rather than a G-2, its nearly circular orbit had a mean radius just enough greater than an Astronomical Unit that its solar flux was nearly identical to Earth's.

The rock bore no life, but its surface was lively. Chains of volcanoes spewed gases into an atmosphere already thick with carbon dioxide and ammonia. Crustal plates collided and shook (ever so slowly), creasing the face of the land.

The rock's barren oceans lay torpid under a warm sun, unstirred by the tides of any moon. Given a few billion years, life might have arisen. But probably not.

Busy men rendered the question meaningless. A large icy comet, nudged from its path by fusion charges, smashed into the rock with such titanic energy that the rock's axis and spin were readjusted. The comet's leftover chunks sped off into a million directions, but one large piece settled into orbit around the planet, providing it with a bright and perfectly serviceable moon.

Microorganisms tailored to the purpose were strewn liberally across the surface of the planet. The reaction was explosive: they ravened upon the carbon dioxide in the air and the carbon dioxide dissolved in the water; they died in prodigious quantities, releasing oxygen, taking carbon with them as they went, in a mineral precipitate that rained heavily upon the ocean floors. The terraformers murdered the carbon fixers before they could go too far; they wanted an atmosphere with an excess of CO_2.

Meanwhile, different strains of laboratory-bred life had been debauching themselves on the nitrogen-rich compounds in the atmosphere. By the time they had poisoned themselves in their own waste they had helped convert the air of the rock to something resembling Earth's, four parts nitrogen to one of oxygen.

Plant forms followed, in forced succession—mosses, lichens, grasses, bushes, trees. Living and dying under hothouse conditions, their wastes and remains built up a thin layer of soil where once there had been only sterile rock and sand.

Just one century passed. The handmade life forms created a planet with a foreordained destiny: to be Earth's breadbasket. Crops were planted in fields as wide as continents. There were grains and fruits and vegetables and fibers, and grasses and legumes and animals to graze on them. There were spices and aromatics, coffees and teas. There was sugar, and there was milk, and honey. In the sea were fishes and shellfishes and crustaceans, and on the mountainsides timber and managed "wild" game. And in the huge greenhouses were a thousand varieties of flowers, mushrooms, what-have-yous, experimental tidbits never conceived by God or Mother Nature.

The rock was christened Bounty. Its flag was the cornucopia.

Earth grew fat and her well-fed billions multiplied.

Among Earth's complacent citizenry a few adventurous souls (not many) complained. They were cheerfully assisted on their way to colonize the living planets of other stars, planets with evolved ecosystems of their own. There they found adventure aplenty; though humans had nowhere yet found or recognized intelligence, alien life sometimes fought back vigorously nonetheless.

But Bounty, Earth's creature, did not resist those who fed upon her.

They never found out where the bugs came from, or why so many kinds showed up at once.

It started with a few varmints that resembled army worms, in a small corner of a big cotton field. The local administrator of the Fiber Board was incensed at what he took to be a personal affront. He had the plants sprayed. The pesticide worked; the pests disappeared.

Next growing season there were six new species of cotton-eater. The combination of chemicals required to kill them was quite effective. It also killed all the fish and shellfish along the adjacent coast.

Before anyone knew what had happened, or could check the wild oscillations of chemical death versus mutant life, a devil's bestiary had attacked the corn, the wheat, the rice, the cows, the pigs, the sheep . . .

Hysteria spread like a prairie fire. There were anguished screams of "sabotage," and indeed, horrible subversive things were found in some private homes: here a potted geranium, there an African violet. People were dragged out and lynched.

There were other theories about the source of the disaster: that a shuttle illegally flushed its tank in the atmosphere, or that the bugs came from space itself on a carbonaceous meteorite, or (the most likely explanation) that they had escaped from Bounty's own laboratories. But no single organism, whether nucleated or non-nucleated, one-celled or many-celled, could have spelled the planet's doom.

That doom was swift, ghastly—the genetic simplicity that had allowed Bounty to be born within a single century now spelled her death in a tenth that time. Several hundred thousand people died, eighty percent of the planet's entire population.

On Earth the fraction was the same. The numbers were unimaginable. And following the deaths due outright to starvation, Earth endured another decade of bloody political upheaval. The New Era was ushered in amid the smoke of a billion funeral pyres; they had burned unquenched for years.

Neither Earth nor Bounty had the will or the means to communicate with the other. Bounty gained unsought independence. On Bounty a new leadership arose from the wreckage, determined to learn the lesson of the holocaust. Eloquent among them was Elizabeth Tanaka, a senior biologist with Central Laboratories, Ceres, the same continent that first noticed the infestation of pests. Tanaka seemed a youthful forty-five or so, an age that would have been confirmed if anyone had consulted the records.

As leaders of the remnant debated their future course,

Tanaka stood forth and delivered a stirring and ultimately decisive address.

From remarks of Citizen Elizabeth Tanaka, Fourth Session. Chamber of Deputies of the Unified Provisional Government of Bounty, on the first day of Primavera, 2180 O.E. (1 N.E.):

"We are guilty of *hubris,* not against any god, but against our own deepest nature. We have forgotten that we are creatures of the natural world, and that all our skill and understanding is as nothing compared to the wisdom inherent in five billion years of blind evolution.

"We must seek our own forgiveness. We must seek to rediscover and recreate the natural order that gave us form, that our pitiful pseudoecology of monocultures has mocked. Though we can create almost any living form we desire, of our own knowledge we can make nothing capable of survival. Only by reconstructing the natural world we have destroyed, reconstructing it in all its complexity throughout time, can we hope to learn again, humbly, what willfully we have forgotten.

"The name 'Bounty' and all the eager exploitation it implies must be wiped from human memory. We must create a new world that honors the processes of nature, the most basic of which is selection.

"We must find a new name to express the deep and subtle understanding we seek, the principle that only the life that is *fitting* can ultimately survive . . ."

8

Holder was in luck. He grinned to himself as he bounced a few centimeters into the air and came back down again, hard, on the steel flooring of the speeding utility buggy. Everything around him bounced in unison: the rusty tackle, the beat-up electric outboard motor and its fuel-cell battery, and the big smelly primitive-looking fish, half teeth, that lay against the buggy's tail gate. Holder was not at all sure the tenacious beast had given up its hold on life; that was one reason he preferred to ride backward at the other end of the truck bed where he could keep an eye on the carcass.

His position had other advantages. Through black ink strokes of jungle shrubbery brushing past overhead and all around him he could see the glimmer of the full moon sailing up from the east. Even as he watched, the shadow of a pteranodon glided across the face of the moon. And in the cab behind his back his benefactors had at least the illusion of privacy. The boy driving was twenty at most, the girl beside him a freckled and sunburned sixteen. Holder hoped that between them they'd manage to keep one hand on the wheel.

He wasn't sure how much of his story they'd bought, the tall tale he'd made up about being lured downriver by a con man and robbed and abandoned, though he'd given them a perfect description of Widefoot Willy, an infamous river rat they'd have recognized. Whether they believed him or not didn't really matter, because if he wasn't a tourist doing a little unauthorized sightseeing (grounds for deportation on Darwin) he was some kind of equivalent outlaw—an off-world skin buyer, maybe. The kids knew he wouldn't be complaining to any Rangers, or talking to anyone about an illegal fish in the back of the six-wheeled buggy.

Holder grinned again, as the buggy walloped through another pothole. He'd saved an entire day—what luck! Even though he wasn't exactly sitting in the lap of luxury, it was better than a sharp stick in the eye, as they said in these parts.

They reached the outskirts of Copeville an hour before midnight. The bushbuggy turned off into a narrow back street leading toward the water, then stopped. Holder clambered down one of the big rubber tires and turned to thank the young Samaritans.

He was taken by the girl's frank brown stare. She gazed at him from the shadows on the far side of the cab with a smoldering look that seemed to tender the elemental secret of life.

Remember your age, Holder.

He tore his gaze from the girl and stepped away. The boy saluted and flashed a mouthful of white teeth; he wheeled his long buggy around in the middle of the road in a centipede's version of a U-turn and barreled off into the moonlit scrub.

For a long time Holder stood alone in the humid night, smelling the heavy perfume of a thousand magnolias, listening to the ratcheting drone of countless frogs. Yellow light spilled across the road from the windows of Whitney's Place, the infamous smugglers' lair. The light projected a shadow play of dancing insects.

Holder walked across the dirt road and up onto the plank porch, which was raised high above ground level to accommodate the Marsh's frequent floods. Whitney's was long, low, and narrow; four people with arms outstretched could reach across it from back to front. That left plenty of room for weekend dances. Though there were screen doors at both ends of the half-block-long porch, Holder knew he must walk the length of it to the door nearest the bar, so the people inside would have a chance to look him over through the screened windows as he approached. Otherwise he could get himself killed by mistake.

He walked slowly, his heels knocking hollowly against the boards. At the thought of coming face to face with Whitney he was taken with a sudden shyness. For the first time he was about to meet someone he knew, not as that person would be in Holder's "now" but as he had been in Holder's "then." Nothing he had done so far in this mad enterprise had so filled him with apprehension.

He took a breath and pushed the creaking door open against its rusty spring.

Whitney was not in sight. Two muscular young dock hands sat hunched over beer glasses at the far end of the bar. One was watching him; thinking he recognized a tourist, he sneered and turned back to his glass.

Farther back in the shadows of the long empty dance hall two older men and a woman played dominoes by the lurid red light of a plastic tyrannosaur, which hung on the unpainted boards of the wall behind them. The beast was rampant, clutching a can of "Dragon's Milk" beer.

Holder smiled when he saw the illuminated sign. He remembered staring at it for long fascinated minutes the first time he'd come into Whitney's, clinging to his father's hand. He'd been five or six years old then, and had not yet seen a live tyrannosaur.

Holder didn't have time to examine the bar's last customer, who sat alone in the dark, for just then Whitney himself emerged from the storeroom behind the bar. It was Whitney all right, long and stringy as a piece of jerky, just as Holder remembered him. Despite Holder's earlier fears, that seemed just as it should.

Whitney stopped when he saw the stranger. He stared guardedly from under beetling, gingery brows, then moved to wipe his hands on the seat of his trousers. Evidently he decided that Holder was not an undercover Ranger (not even a fink would lower himself to dress like a *tourist*), for when he brought his hands out from behind his back he held no weapon.

"Evenin', mister," Whitney said, almost whispering. "Want somethin'?"

Holder hitched himself onto a bar stool in the folksy manner of a tourist imitating a local. "How about a beer?" he suggested cheerfully, pushing his broad-brimmed safari hat to the back of his head.

"We got Dragon's Milk, 'n we got Palm," Whitney croaked.

Before he could answer, Holder heard a heavy footstep behind him. "Do ask for Palm, for Gawd's sake," drawled a loud voice.

The men at the bar turned, reacting with undisguised contempt, curious to see how Holder would respond to a character they knew well. But the hairs rose on the back of Holder's neck. The voice was unmistakably familiar, a fruity British accent Holder happened to know had been acquired in Saint Cloud, Minnesota.

He had not expected and had not wanted to hear that voice for at least another day.

Holder wheeled around on the bar stool. A florid fat man stood before him, sweating profusely. Holder knew the face as well as his own: shiny cheeks, matted red ringlets of hair, lips of baby Eros. And so young! Thirty, at most. Somehow Holder had not been prepared for that—he'd always thought of this man as much older than himself.

The ersatz Britisher stared back at him. "Awfully sorry,

my good fellow. I'd no intention of giving you such a fright." He moved toward the stool beside Holder's, then hesitated. "D'you mind?"

Holder recovered. "Not at all. Please."

The fat young man draped his ample bottom over the stool and leaned toward Holder familiarly. "Dragon's Milk, indeed," he harrumphed. "Dragon's piss, more likely. At least Palm's drinkable."

Holder turned back to Whitney. "Palm it is."

Whitney reached into the cooler and pulled out two bottles of Palm. "Four cents," he hissed, holding fast to the bottles.

The fat man stared at the bottles, flicking his tongue over rosebud lips. Then he fumbled in the pockets of his jacket. "Here somewhere, quite certain of that."

"Allow me," Holder said, after a slightly indecent pause. He handed Whitney a plastic blank yellowed with age.

Whitney took it suspiciously, still clinging to the sweating bottles with one hand. The blank looked positively ancient, though it bore contemporary edge markings. Meanwhile the fat man had instantly stopped searching his pockets. A look of relief spread over his shiny round features. "I say, that's really too good of you. . . ."

"I know," said Holder, reflecting that he had indeed learned a lot from this man.

To Whitney's evident surprise the aged piece of plastic was perfectly legitimate. His bar terminal registered four cents.

". . . and I do appreciate it," said the fat man. "Unwin's the name, T.T. Unwin. And yours, sir?"

Holder took the credit blank from Whitney and shoved it back in his blouse pocket. "What's the 'T' for?" he asked.

"Which T?" Unwin asked defensively.

"Either. Both."

"My father was a classical scholar," said Unwin with a sign. "Oxford, you know. The full name is Telemachus Teucer Unwin."

In spite of himself Holder grinned sadistically. "Named you after a couple of Greek archers, eh? Tell me, T.T., does your shaft always hit the mark?"

Unwin looked acutely uncomfortable. In a very low voice he said, "Don't tell me that my face has, aah, spread itself before me?"

"People say I'm a regular mind reader."

"It is indeed a pleasure to meet another cultivated man,

I must say." Unwin attempted a smile, but only managed to appear shifty. "But you really do have the advantage of me, sir."

"Smith. John Smith. Why don't you call me Smith?" Holder extended his hand.

Unwin took the proffered hand with limp enthusiasm. "As you will—Mister Smith."

The touch of Unwin's moist flesh gave Holder an indescribably queasy sensation. He snatched his hand away and wrapped it around his beer bottle. Both men drank. Both were practiced at it; before the bottles hit the bar again half of each had disappeared. Unwin was right about the beer, thought Holder. He'd forgotten how good Palm was. And he'd earned his today.

Now what in the world was he going to do about Unwin? Damn it! What was Unwin doing here *early?* "What brings you to Cretacia, T.T.?" Holder asked, awfully casually.

"Pursuit of learning, *Mister* Smith." Unwin sniffed. "You see before you a wandering scholar, a student of human nature, not to mention many abstruse disciplines both philosophical and, especially, mathematical." Unwin belched, then sighed. "Also, alas, practical . . . from time to time I am forced to seek sustenance in the form of a paying job." Unwin sucked thoughtfully on his beer.

"Any immediate prospects?"

"Why yes, in fact." Unwin sounded pleased with himself. "Chief Ranger Holder has advertised for a tutor for his lad. A most compassionate father, that—doesn't want to banish the boy to a boarding school. I caught wind of the offer, and wired the man a *vitae* from my hotel in Cuvier. He was impressed, of course. In turn he invited me for an interview—wired me passage, too."

"Congratulations," Holder said mechanically. He knew it all to the letter. He knew the name of Unwin's hotel in Cuvier, and he knew that Unwin's accommodations there consisted entirely of a message-intercept service provided by an epicene desk clerk whose flat Unwin was sharing.

What was the man saying?

". . . airship here, and by boat to Waterhouse tomorrow. Then, assuming all goes well, thence to Holder's jungle stockade, or wherever he lives, on the day after."

"Tomorrow?" Holder looked at Unwin with surprise.

"Ghastly business, what? But one must eat."

"You're going to Waterhouse tomorrow?" Holder repeated.

"Quite so," said Unwin a bit suspiciously. "If I may be so bold, Smith, what's it to you?"

"What's today's date?" Holder blurted.

"Why, the fourteenth of Tri, I believe. Oneday night." Unwin glanced at his wrist unit. "Almost Twoday morning, actually."

Seeing the fat man's puzzled expression Holder realized he'd better make some excuse. "The river boat runs tomorrow, does it? Must have heard them wrong at the hotel—could have missed the trip." Holder took a long swig of beer, trying to hide his confusion. The dates were right but the events were in the wrong place; there was a definite discrepancy, unless he'd made some error in his historical reconstruction. Unwin was not even supposed to *arrive* in Copeville for two more days.

"So you'll be going to Waterhouse too?" Unwin asked. "They say it's posh. Rather wish I was staying on . . . not striking out for the interior right away." Wistfully he swallowed the remaining quarter of his beer, then turned a hopeful eye on Holder's.

Holder polished off his bottle. "It's late," he said sternly, banging the empty bottle against the bar. "Time to get some rest. I'll walk you to the hotel."

"That really is too kind," Unwin mourned.

Holder stood up and without a backward glance walked out the door.

Whether because of Holder's commanding voice, or (more likely) because of his own temporarily depleted resources, the pudgy Unwin waddled after him.

Holder heard Unwin come out behind him, and he could feel the baleful eyes of the denizens of Whitney's, staring at the backs of both their necks.

9

. . . requires you urgently pursue line of inquiry outlined by your communication earlier today. Recent top security investigations at FRAME Corporation and elsewhere (pertinent sections appended below) confirm theoretical feasibility of travel mode you suggest. Consider Holder possible Darwinian agent. Note Darwinian fascination with history, per SecServ whitefile appended below. Be aware of possible extreme danger to the status quo. Speaker Macklin requires you report progress twice daily.

This is a big one, Angel. Ted is depending on you for this one.

Best,
Bicknell

Appendix One: biographical data, suspect Unwin (per ref. S. Jerome int, this date) . . .

Professor Telemachus Teucer Unwin tugged at a lock of his curly grey hair (it retained a tinge of copper still) and sucked in his rosebud lips. His cheeks were still cherubic, though his sixty-plus years had spread a fine net of wrinkles across them, and his eyes gleamed with a sly look that time had accentuated, not softened.

Angelica Claymore watched him with her own dark, steady eyes. She seemed willing to wait as long as it took for him to begin talking.

Despite his acute sense of danger, Unwin could not help thinking that Claymore bore a remarkable resemblance to the Mona Lisa, at least in this setting. She was seated in perfect repose, her hands folded in her lap, while behind her the tall tinted windows of the Medical School library admitted a pearly light, nicely balanced by the light from the interior fixtures. Through the fiftieth-floor windows one could see a distant landscape of sea and headlands, rendered painterly by the smoky glass.

Unwin let a little puff of air escape his pursed lips. "There's a saying that was common in the late Industrial Age, Officer Claymore, that perfectly expresses my personal philosophy."

"Yes?"

" 'I'd rather have a bottle in front of me—than a frontal lobotomy.' "

Claymore smiled. "You have nothing to fear, Professor."

Unwin sighed. He didn't believe her for a moment, but what could he do? His only hope lay in cooperation. "Poor deranged Phil Holder," he began, turning his sigh of resignation into one of feigned regret. "He *did* talk to me on a number of occasions before his final excursion, though I must stress that we were not close friends, not by any means —frankly, I think he never did like me—and of course I'm delighted to share the contents of those discussion with you, an authorized representative of the Federal Government. But I would be most distressed—indeed, devastated—if you were to confuse Holder's mad ideas with my own rather, aah, mundane views."

"The Persian messenger syndrome, is that it, Professor?"

"A frightened man is not a reliable witness."

She was still smiling, but her words weren't friendly. "You suggest I spare your brain, for the sake of accurate information."

Unwin spread his fingers and shrugged. But damn the woman!

With a pointed fingernail Claymore probed the intricately embroidered pattern of her genuine silk jacket. "What is an appropriate ransom for a man's mind?"

What indeed? "Your assurance, at least . . ." Unwin began.

"You have it," she said quickly. "As a representative of the Federal Government, I am of course bound by the Constitution, . . ."

(What the hell does that mean? Is she mocking me?)

". . . so please tell me everything you have to say, Professor." Incredibly, she was still smiling.

He had hoped to make her drag it out of him, thus increasing the apparent value of the information. But just then she looked at him in a way he could not have described. He felt an urge to talk.

"Time travel!" he blurted. "That's what Phil was trying to do. Travel back in time." (There! That should give her something to think about.)

Claymore's left eyebrow lifted slightly, but her smile never wavered.

Desperately, Unwin rushed on. "He didn't mean to go far, about thirty years, only back to when he was a boy of thirteen. Why was he doing it, you ask?" (She hadn't, but he knew she would.) "I'm not sure quite how to put it. He wanted to, aah, he wanted to prevent himself from living the life he has, in fact, led."

Claymore continued to watch him calmly, but for the first time the smile slipped and the faintest look of puzzlement creased her brow. "You mean growing younger, recovering his youth?"

"No, that's impossible." Hastily he added, "I mean, that's even *more* impossible. I mean, he didn't believe that was possible." Unwin stopped for breath. "He knew there would be two of him," he resumed. "He wanted to find himself as a boy, and, aah, influence that boy. That earlier version of himself."

Claymore's smile at last disappeared altogether.

Unwin was encouraged. "Perhaps I was mistaken when I assumed your omniscience, Officer? Did you know I was Holder's tutor when he was a boy?"

"I know that. I know quite a few things about you."

"Mmm, no doubt. But that was the point of his journey, don't you see?"

"What point?" Claymore demanded.

"He's fired me in retrospect!" Momentarily Unwin forgot his fear. He chuckled. "He's gone back to do the job himself. He thinks *he* can do it right!"

Claymore was silent, brooding.

Unwin was unsure what he'd said that had unsettled her. She'd showed no surprise when he'd mentioned the concept of time travel itself.

Finally she spoke. "I'm afraid you'll have to do better, Professor."

"Better?" He was sincerely surprised.

"No one would go to such lengths just to alter his *personal* history."

"But people do it all the time," Unwin protested. "Vicariously, anyway. Those who are allowed to have children try to live their lives over again through them, I mean."

She ignored this. "What could the man have done, so evil that he became obsessed with undoing it?"

Unwin shrugged. His eyes wandering to the galleries where students studied with earphones and projectors, lost in worlds of their own. "True, Holder's share of evil seems as banal as most. One can scarcely imagine it living after him. Nevertheless, it is not inconsiderable. Whose is?"

Claymore's eyes flashed. "Don't waste my time with riddles."

Suddenly Unwin was terribly afraid. Something told him Claymore was in an awful hurry, her seeming calm notwithstanding. Brainburning might be the lesser of his worries. He made up his mind to tell her everything she asked; he leaned toward her and spoke rapidly, sincerely. "Holder believed he doomed everyone he cared about; that's what drove him. And he had reason! His second wife, that's what started him thinking about it—they were trying to decide whether they could live through a second triad, and they'd decided they could. They went to Amor on a second honeymoon, to celebrate. The first night they were there they argued while out walking. He headed for a bar, she started back to their hotel. She was murdered. The motive was robbery, presumably."

A look of distaste crossed Claymore's face. "How do you know this?"

"I . . . everybody . . . he told me," Unwin spluttered. "He told me all about it. It's what started him wondering about what happened to his *first* wife." Unwin raced on. "She was, to put it bluntly, deranged. A simple organic problem, most likely; no one will ever know. Holder refused to recognize it—well, he was hardly more than a boy. But his wife and baby son disappeared in the wreck of the *Griffin,* while *he* survived. Holder told me he was sure she was the one who was responsible for the wreck." Unwin broke off.

There was a strange expression on Claymore's face. "The *Griffin?* Holder's wife was on the *Griffin*? With Ruiz? And *Ted Macklin?*"

Unwin could only nod, captivated by the intensity of Claymore's stare.

"And *he* thinks *she did it . . .* ?"

Unwin stared back at her.

Claymore leaned to her briefcase and came up with a file-slab. She held it close to Unwin's face and pushed its stud; a reedy voice issued untranscribed from the miniature speaker: "*. . . one never emerges in the same spacetime one leaves . . .*"

Claymore spoke over the voice from the slab. "If you want me to spare your precious brain, Professor, help me find out whose voice is on this slab. And fast."

Unwin licked his lips. "As you wish, Officer. I place myself under your protection."

10

The *Marsh Queen* skittered down the launching ramp, rubber skirts aflap, and floundered noisily onto the broad bosom of the river. From the shallows a family of titanosaurs watched, munching on vegetation plucked from the swampy shore. With their long necks arcing in concentric curves, the family of sauropods made a considerably more graceful sight than the old hovercraft, until at last the craft picked up enough speed to skate swiftly and surely away across the surface of the water, heading downstream for Copeville.

From the top floor balcony of Waterhouse, a kilometer from the wharf, Holder watched the riverboat leave. A few small groups of tourists shared the wide observation platform with him, but they were far more interested in dinosaur-spotting than in the departing boat. Only one man, darkly bearded and flashily dressed in Eridanian silks, seemed unimpressed by the scenery; he seemed more interested in Holder, but looked casually away when Holder glanced in his direction. Holder had never seen him before, and paid him no attention.

The resort hotel stood high on polysteel posts cast to imitate great tree trunks a dozen meters tall, high enough to raise it up among the real trees and above the stagnant humidity of the swamp. As far as Holder's eye could see, green trees draped with vines towered among still pools of water. The pools reflected a soft blue sky with scattered downy clouds. The flat world of water and plants stretched away on all sides; only to the west was the horizon broken by a string of eroded volcanoes. Beyond them, higher and hazier still, stood the immense cone of Mount Owen, crowned with a column of smoke and steam, a perpetual shadow against heaven.

Holder shaded his eyes and peered west, into the glare of the late afternoon sun. From the gorge of the Marsh, where it bent north to skirt the great volcano, Chief Ranger Alexander Holder, Administrative Director of Upper and Lower Cretacia, would soon be coming downriver to meet "T.T. Unwin."

Getting rid of the real Unwin had, happily, proved to be as easy as Holder had hoped, despite the upset caused by the anomalous slippage in dates. That first night, on the road between Whitney's and the Copeville hotel, Holder had socked T.T. with a one-two punch. Blackmail first—on Darwin, a planet obsessed with the reproductive function, even a hint of same-sex preference was cause for ostracism.

... years in the most primitive, reptile-infested area of the whole primitive continent. No cultivated companions. Ranger Holder's a bluff, hearty type, not your sort really, and gone most of the time anyway. And his wife is worse: dull, and a savage moralist. Five years in the jungle! And only the boy to keep you company... Frankly, Unwin, I'm surprised you were—will be, that is—able to resist temptation for as long as five years...

And second, bribery—using a significant portion of Holder's last research grant, perhaps a megacent's worth of credit recorded on a thin sliver of blue plastic.—*I told you it was a perfect crime, Unwin; it won't be committed for another 30 years yet—*

"That's ridiculous," Unwin assured him, but he'd pocketed the sliver anyway, and by now he was on his way to Epsilon Eridani, a rich if thoroughly confused, young man.

Far off on the silvery river Holder detected movement, a black dot skimming the water at high speed, spreading a thin rapid wake behind it: the airboat.

The airboat would take at least an hour to reach Waterhouse. Holder ran his tongue over lips that suddenly felt dry. He'd been good about alcohol for an incredibly long time now, hadn't he? But every once in a while the thirst hit him—as now, with his father on the way. Already in sight, in fact. A father younger than himself.

The thought made his head reel. Not the thought, really, for he'd contemplated the situation often enough; it was the awful imminence . . .

He laughed aloud, suddenly, nervously. After all he'd been through and done, to get drunk and flunk the interview!

He glanced around to see if anyone had noticed his lapse of self control, but the tourists were all gathered at the far end of the deck, exclaiming at the sight of a group of domeheads wallowing in the shallows. The black-bearded man was casually studying the clouds.

Holder could wait. By the time the airboat docked and the Ranger made his way to the hotel it would be getting on toward sunset. His father had never minded a drink.

Yes, he'd wait. He'd think about something else until then.

11

". . . from the point of view of someone left behind, a ship falling into a black hole is falling into the future. It doesn't look that way, since the light returning from the departing ship is violently red-shifted, just the way ancient distant objects are red-shifted. But in fact the hole's gravity accelerates an infalling object to near light speed. As velocity increases, time—relative to the observer left behind—dilates. And if that ship were to return . . .

". . . we observe that ships and radio messages make black hole transits frequently, yet manage to stay loosely within a 'present' that can be agreed upon by Earth and Darwin and Ichtiaque and Epsilon Eridani and Brindle and Tau Ceti and all the other worlds of the Starry Archipelago. Fast ships,

because of their proper velocities, are forever adjusting their clocks to the local standard, and the calculation of arrival and departure times is a not unsubtle art. But the black hole Stations themselves—which should distort time as they distort space, spacetime being a seamless manifold—add no complications whatever. This was an amazing and inexplicable phenomenon to the earliest explorers . . .

". . . Walker found it convenient to posit a region of superspace where time runs backwards. Walker, of course, had no reason to suppose he was describing reality—he simply needed a term to make his equations balance. In the arbitrary Walkerian scheme a ship approaching a black hole supposedly sets up a potential time differential, a delta tau in superspace. This potential is discharged as the ship leaps the hyperfold and re-enters the ordinary universe. Delta tau plus should match delta tau minus. And it appears to. But does it really . . . ?

". . . consider antimatter. For every kind of particle there is a corresponding antiparticle. Yet the ordinary world is constructed almost entirely of ordinary matter. In nature, antimatter is found only in rare deposits, locked in the quark structure of the superhydrogens, as in the 'super-ice' glaciers of Brindle. But why should not antimatter exist in the same proportions as ordinary matter throughout the universe? Why are there no antiplanets, antistars, antigalaxies? Physicists have long been accustomed to treating antiparticles in two different but equivalent ways—as particles with reversed charge or spin or magnetic moment relative to their ordinary particle mate, or as the ordinary particle itself traveling backways in time. . . .

". . . do whole anti-universes exist, segregated from us by a time sense opposed to our own, unable to communicate because their messages arrive before they are sent, coded in mirror gibberish on receding waves? Do drowsy Maxwell's demons guard the black hole gates between these universes and our own, assigned to keep everything separate but nodding off now and then and allowing the reversed particles to slip through . . . ?

". . . count the points on a line: an infinity. Count the points on a plane: a greater infinity. Count the points in a three-space: a greater infinity still. Now count the lines in a plane, the planes in a three-space, the three-spaces in superspace . . .

". . . maintain symmetry. Assume as many time-reversed universes as time-normal universes. The number of each is infinite . . .

". . . assume the origin of all universes in a Big Bounce. Assume the end of all universes in a Big Bounce. Mark each Bounce on an abscissa, and connect them with a smooth curve—above the line, time-normal universes, below the line, time-reversed. Now recall that a sine wave graphs a closed curve . . .

". . . consider our presumption of instantaneous travel a shared illusion. One never emerges in the same spacetime one leaves—hence those tiny shifts in the phenomenal world we travelers of the universe have come to know so well. Are the freckles on your lover's nose slightly askew since last you said goodbye? There are a million billion yous, an infinity of yous, and you have a million billion lovers. What orgies of rediscovery all travelers might enjoy, if only they knew . . ."

Claymore switched off the fileslab she held in her hand. "Your voice?"

"We knew that you—or someone like you—would find us sooner or later, Officer. We're not professional conspirators." The woman was small, trim, spare; her salt-and-pepper hair was cut close to her head. The only light in Unwin's office came from a single desk lamp aimed down at the papers on his desk. Claymore could not determine the woman's age, for she kept her face in shadow.

"The fake ident on this slab is hardy the work of an amateur," Claymore said coolly.

"We are not amateur programmers," the woman replied. "But, unfortunately for us, that bit of fakery was a woefully inadequate afterthought—when we realized it was already too late to erase the memo to Phil."

Unwin stood dejectedly in the corner near the door, looking crumpled, as if he'd been discarded there. "We had absolutely no idea Phil was going to *use* that . . ."

Claymore's look silenced him. "I find, Professor, that you give me more useful information when I ask you direct questions."

"Aah, mmm," Unwin agreed.

His office was little more than a cubbyhole on the thirty-second floor of Parnassus, its modesty reflecting the secondary importance to the Medical School of its mathematics department. It was an outside room, though, with a view east across the floating suburbs—flickering dull yellow lights in the smoky darkness—to the tall glowing soleris in the hills on the far shore. On the otherwise dark flatlands of both shores bonfires burned, kindled from trash and old planks ripped from the sides of undefended houses.

"Amateurs or not, you have conspired to conceal evidence of a felony. And perhaps worse."

"We're eager to have you understand what Phil was doing," the woman said. "Then you'll know the theft of that lander was his only crime."

"Everyone I've met is dedicated to apologizing for poor Philip Holder." Claymore allowed her temper to show. "Unwin here has apologized for him at length. Holder only wanted to atone for his sins, is that it, Unwin?"

"Mmm, aah . . ."

"I'm not referring to his motives," the woman said, with a touch of asperity. "I'm speaking of methods. I'm talking about the laws of the physical world. Once you understand those, you'll understand that Holder represents no further threat to anyone in this universe."

"You too want to claim he's dead?"

"Not at all, though he probably is. You've studied our memo. You've studied the abstracts it contains, all the way back to Walker and Wheeler and Hoyle. You know that if Phil succeeded in traveling back in time, he's in another universe entirely, one that has no causal connction with our own."

"A mathematical convenience, not a fact," said Claymore. "By that reasoning, we should change universes every time we pass through black hole Stations, whether we're attempting to time-travel or not."

The small woman in the shadows said nothing. Meanwhile Unwin nervously murmured something inaudible.

"Well?" said Claymore, exasperated. "That's absurd, isn't it? The laws of cause and effect demonstrably operate between here and Darwin. They operate now, and they operated in the past, and they always will."

"Have you ever actually traveled to another star, Officer?" the woman asked. "Relatively few people have."

"I made a trip to Brindle once," Claymore replied. (That had been lovely—so much emptiness. But her work was on Earth.)

"Since you returned from Brindle," asked the woman, "have you looked at any pictures of yourself made before you left?" Her face came into the dim yellow reflected light of the desk lamp; it was an old face, remarkably old for Earth.

(*. . . are the freckles on your lover's nose slightly askew since last you said goodbye . . .?*)

A *frisson* of horror prickled Claymore's arms. "You're saying the Earth I'm standing on now, here in this room, is not the same Earth I left?"

"The mathematical expressions we are discussing require that Officer Claymore's Doppelgänger left this Earth at the same moment Officer Claymore herself—you—left whatever Earth you came from. A complicated hypothesis, but it suggests some simple tests. For example, look at an old holo of yourself, and then in the mirror. It's quite possible that random quantum events at the cellular level have produced tiny changes in your appearance that only you would recognize."

For a moment Claymore chose not to doubt the outcome of such an experiment. "Which of us would be real?" she asked quietly.

"You are real, of course. Could I persuade you otherwise? Unwin over there is real, I'm real—reality is experience. Just as proper time is the time where you are, so proper reality is the reality where you are." The woman paused a moment, and then added as if it were an afterthought, "Of course all the Doppelgängers are real too."

(*A million billion yous, an infinity of yous . . .*)

The thought dizzied Claymore; she pushed it away, changing the subject. "I want to leave the mathematics aside a moment . . ."

"You can't leave the mathematics aside," said the woman.

Claymore persisted. ". . . long enough to hear about the mechanics."

The woman sighed impatiently, then said rapidly, "We knew the precise velocity of *Humboldt* at superspace insertion, barring accident; we knew the precise mass of the stolen lander; we knew a number of other parameters. The problem was how to delay the lander's passage through the hyperfold—and how *long* to delay it. The longer the transition, the greater the value of *tau minus. Humboldt* emerged in the so-called present. The lander, staying in the fold the merest fraction of a second longer, emerged thirty years earlier."

Claymore was silent a moment, staring out the window at the smoky night. At last she said, "You'll do the same for me."

"We'll be glad to show you the calculations we did."

"No! *New* calculations. Based on a new Darwin transit. I'll be able to give you the details by morning. The ship will be Sprint class; we'll equip it however you recommend."

"But whatever *for?*" Unwin protested.

"I intend to pursue Holder and eliminate the threat he represents," Claymore told him.

"He represents no threat whatsoever!" Unwin sounded genuinely shocked.

"He can change the course of history."

"Some other history, perhaps. This reality is already what it is."

"Whether he means to or not," Claymore finished.

The old woman intervened. "Officer Claymore, experience suggests that when a mathematical construct accurately predicts events in the real world, it is to some degree 'true.' Our construct posits the generation of all possible universes simultaneously, not as a uniquely determined outcome, but as a set of probabilities—like a wave packet, a wave of waves. Our wave packet can be treated as a single entity, a 'slice of life,' 'relaton,' if you will—but only by experiencing its precise properties directly at any given moment. We all constantly sample reality, and in the act of sampling, determine what is real for us in our universe."

"And we know damned well Phil Holder didn't do what he said he was going to in *this* reality," said Unwin huffily. "I'd have known about it, *directly*. And another thing—if you go after him, how are you going to manage to end up in the same place *he* did? There are a *million billion* alternatives, remember? An *infinity* of alternatives."

"Which 'he,' Unwin?" Claymore asked, acidly. "By your model there are an infinity of Holders, too. Even if *some* of them succeeded in altering *some* realities, we could hear about it from the very next ship that comes back through Earth Station."

"Impossible!" Unwin was almost shouting now, pushing his bulk forward into the dark cramped space to confront Claymore. "You have not grasped the nature of the directional bias that . . ."

"Of course the possibility is vanishingly small," the old

woman mused, interrupting Unwin as if he had not spoken.
Unwin froze, open-mouthed. "What are you saying, Clarissa?" He struggled to regain his composure. "It was *you* who argued that significant changes can accumulate only in neighboring . . ."
"Nevertheless . . ." the woman began.
But Unwin, betrayed, would not listen; he turned on Claymore, his dignity restored by anger. "Follow Holder if you wish, Officer. But let me warn you, it takes a suicide to make the attempt. We know for a fact that most of those infinite Holders *didn't* succeed—the man who might have landed in our past, for one. Holder knew the odds too. If you follow him you'll share those odds. You'll end up where he did. I happen to think that's nowhere, and I do mean Nowhere."
"Your accent has disappeared, Professor," Claymore said.
Unwin smiled, but he looked ghastly. "Some of your Doppelgängers will doubtless get through. Is that any comfort?"
"Will it comfort you, Professor? You realize I need to be reassured as to the accuracy of your calculations; and so, of course, you must come with me, you and Professor Sirich."

12

"Her critics to the contrary, Tanaka was always acutely aware of the seeming paradox of Darwin: that of an institution dedicated to the study of adaptive change, which pursued those studies by attempting to recreate and preserve a collection of separated, static environments.

"But Tanaka always maintained that it was best to try to understand one thing at a time. First, she said, we must learn the construction of the individual organisms themselves. Second, through a kind of vital mimesis we must learn to construct complex stable ecosystems typical of those which existed at various times in the history of Earth—a process that could well require centuries. Only then could we hope to control the complex variables of ecosystem change.

"Not surprisingly, Tanaka took a leading role in shaping the Uniform Code of Natural Human Life, the major thrust of which was to halt tendencies toward uncontrolled artificial evolution of the human organism. At the time only a very few people knew that Tanaka herself was in heinous violation of several of the Code's most basic tenets, including those against direct intervention with the underlying metabolic processes and those against permanent alteration of the reproductive organs.

"Elizabeth Tanaka lived to the ripe old age of eighty-five years (Standard) before arranging to have herself expire. We may note in passing that the woman born Margaret Tanner subsequently appeared under four different guises during the course of the next century (see Notes in Appendix III for biographical details) before assuming the identity by which, as fate would have it, she became known to posterity—that of Clarissa Sirich. . . ."

(from *Darwin: A Millennium of Conservation*)

On Earth they had begun saving genetic samples in the last quarter of the 20th century, when the imminent collapse of genetic diversity had become clearly apparent. The wild strains were preserved as a hedge against the miscarriage of man's laboratory wonders. Optimists thought they would be useful to maintain arboretums and zoos; only pessimists thought they would ever be needed for any serious purpose.

Thus the pioneers of Darwin had a relatively easy time, several centuries later, reconstructing the plains of East Africa, the tundra of North America, or the Australian desert *ca.* 1850 O.E.

The latter epochs of the Tertiary period provided an interesting challenge, though in many cases refined Amosov-Cole techniques could be used on actual frozen or mummified tissue samples.

The Mesozoic era was much more challenging, for there were very few organic remains to be imported from Earth: a few insects in amber, an occasional carbon "copy" left when an animal had disappeared leaving behind only its cellular carbon, or here and there perhaps a bit of much-altered bone. Most of what survived was stone analogue—skeletons, fossilized skin, the imprint of scales or feathers, petrified footprints. Animals from before the Cenozoic had to be recreated from scratch.

Knowing approximate age and evolutionary lineage, a genetic engineer could specify the proteins presumed to constitute the animal, and the exact sequence of their amino acids. Known proteins were synonymous with known genes; known constellations of protein implied known control genes.

But the "one gene, one protein" approach had gone out of fashion a couple of decades after the elucidation of the structure of DNA—it was over-simplified and inadequate to explain (among other things) morphology. The shapes of closely related animals often differ far more than their protein sequences would suggest, and animals that look very much alike often have widely divergent structural genes.

Picture a sequence of animal skeletons—different, but related through evolutionary time—as frames of an animated film. When projected, the film would show bones stretching, contracting, growing thick or thin, appearing here and expanding, contracting there and disappearing—with continuity evident throughout. That the forms of related plants and animals change over time, that species are extinguished and new species arise while the basic continuity of life goes on, was evident to several thinkers before Charles Darwin. So plastic did life appear that most pre-Darwinian evolutionists thought the evolutionary mechanism must be simple, and fairly fast-acting—perhaps animals could change shape merely by taking thought!

Plastic dinosaurs are plastic only from the god-like perspective that squeezes tens of millions of years of evolution into a few seconds. But such is the perspective of an ordinary Genetic Engineer Grade 18 (specialty: ornithischia/saurischia). Already equipped with a catalogue of protein- and protein-control genes, his tool kit was made complete by a sophisticated set of so-called morphogens unknown to earlier ages. The morphogens were not mysterious substances in themselves; rather they were complicated assemblies of known hormones and other simple chemicals whose function was controlled by even more complex genetic timing sequences. Yet once these timing sequences had been mastered, basic animal structures could be shaped to any final form the engineer desired. Take the standard vertebrate forelimb—it could be shaped *in* (vitrous) *utero* into a bat's or a bird's wing, a dolphin's flipper or a frog's webbed forefoot, a bear's claw or a monkey's hand or a horse's hoof. Indeed, the engineer could grow human hands on a chicken, or wings on a woman. None ever tried it, on Darwin—the penalty for deliberately creating a monster was exile.

Several decades passed while Darwin's genetic engineers mastered morphogenic techniques. Meanwhile planetary engineers completed a task that was conceptually simpler, but staggering in practice—the sterile isolation of one geological age (the reserved continent or sub-continent) from all others. For big land animals, wide bodies of water and high mountain walls were enough. But to keep flying and swimming and climbing and drifting things apart, impenetrable barriers as deep as oceans and as high as the sky were needed. These barriers were created from diverse materials according to need: here currents of warm or cold air and water, there impermeable glass dams; here permanent flows of molten lava, there permanent chains of electrical storms; here a simple electrical fence, there beams of deadly radiation or poison gas or acid rain. Over ninety-nine percent of its surface, Darwin was the Garden of Eden; here and there it was hell.

At last all was ready. The institute for Biological Research was dedicated in the planetary capital of Cuvier, and the wandering visitor could find inscriptions here and there, carved into odd niches of the polysteel stonework, suitable to the work going on inside. One read:

> *The biologist is in the position of an archaeologist who uncovers a machine without any written record and attempts to reconstruct not only its operation but also its purpose.*
>
> —Richard C. Lewontin, 1978 O.E.

Immediately below was the bold postscript:

> *Often it is necessary to reconstruct the machine first.*
>
> —Elizabeth Tanaka, 11 N.E.

But inside the Institute, where no casual visitor was likely to see them or comprehend them if he did, a great many other inscriptions were written, using a different typeface, a more restricted alphabet, and an altogether different language—for example, these instructions for the assembly of *Tyrannosaurus rex:*

GGAAAGCGGGCAGTCAGCGCAACGCAATTAATGTGAGTTAGCTC
CCTTTCGCCCGTCAGTCGCGTTGCGTTAATTACACTCAATCGAG

ACTCATTAGGCACCCCAGCCTTTACACTTTATGCTTCCCGCTCG
TGAGTAATCCGTGGGGTCGGAAATGTGAAATACGAAGGGCGAGC

TATGTTGTGTGGTTAATTGTGAGCGGGATAACAATTTCACACAG
ATACAACACACCAATTAACACTCACCCTATTGTTAAAGTGTGTC

GAAACA
CTTTGT...

(and so forth, for roughly a million pages.)

13

"You're sure I don't know you, Unwin?" the Chief Ranger demanded, squinting hard. "You look damned familiar." The rays of the setting sun shone fully on Alex Holder's dark, smooth-shaven face.

Philip Holder choked back the irrational panic knocking at his throat. Alex Holder was an impressive man, impressive enough to scare hell out of his son, even though he was much shorter than Philip Holder remembered him—and even though the son was now eight years older than his "old man." But his father could not possibly imagine the truth. "I'm sure we've never met. I must have one of those faces."

"Must have. You look a lot older than I thought you would, too. What's a man your age doing at loose ends?" The Chief Ranger took a deep swallow of his rye, keeping an eye on Holder over the rim of his glass.

"I was on sabbatical, Ranger, from the Math Department at Epseridan U. And frankly, I fell in love with my freedom.

I decided to see a little more of the universe before I locked myself up in a classroom again. Before I knew it, I found myself, aah, embarrassed for funds." (A bowdlerized version of Unwin's real adventures, thought Holder, but Dad bought it—that other time.)

"I sound brusque, Unwin?" The Ranger's expression softened somewhat. "Sorry. Been spending too much time back in the bush." He held up his empty glass and rattled the ice cubes. "Have another?"

"Don't mind if I do," Holder said huskily.

"You too, Frank," Alex said to the sinewy, sun-blackened man, also in Ranger's uniform, who sat with them at the outdoor table. "On the company." Without waiting for the man's reply the Chief Ranger waved three spatulate fingers toward Waterhouse's innkeeper, who'd been keeping the Holder party in view while serving the other guests on the observation deck.

Cobb, the innkeeper, nodded in Alex's direction. There were no helots on Darwin, and most Darwinians were proud and independent, even those who dealt professionally with tourists all the time. Alex Holder got a touch of extra service nonetheless, since Waterhouse operated at his sufferance. Offworlders were permitted this far up the river but no further, except in small, closely supervised tour groups—lest they be crushed or eaten by dinosaurs, or worse, somehow upset the delicate experimental ecology of Upper Cretacia.

For a moment the three men were silent, watching the evening unfold. The low sun backlit the shapes of huge reptiles gliding across the metallic sheen of the swamp. Palms and hardwoods stood up orange and black against the purple sunset sky. Far off, over the treetops, pteranodons wheeled. The scene was almost too vivid, like a set for a musical sensie.

The reptilian swimmers were a family of titanosaurs (big, but smaller than their name suggested), who poled their bodies across the shallow swamp by reaching their forelegs down to the bottom mud. They held their heads high and let their hind legs and tails float along behind them.

The taciturn Seaton broke the silence. "Big female in the middle's the same one got away from that three-year-old rex last monsoon. You recall, Alex? She drew him into quicksand."

The Ranger snorted. "Do I recall? Mamaka told me we almost lost the copter, pulling him out."

Seaton nodded. "Yes, that's her. See the scars above the shoulder? Teeth. She was lucky."

The innkeeper appeared with the drinks and set them on the plank table.

"Thanks, Mr. Cobb," said the Ranger.

"My pleasure, Alex," said the big affable innkeeper. "By the way, I've reserved the Iguanodon for you and your party, if you're interested."

Alex laughed. "Why not? Unwin here will get a kick out of it."

Phil Holder pretended to be puzzled.

With a broad smile wrinkling his square face, Cobb explained. "Our establishment takes its name from the very first man who ever had a go at restoring dinosaurs, Mr. Unwin. His name was Waterhouse Hawkins, and he lived in England back in O.E., in the 19th century. In those days the iguanodon was about the only complete skeleton they'd found, and Hawkins made some life-sized models of the beast for the Crystal Palace exhibition."

"Pretty good models, too," Alex Holder put in, "considering. Course they didn't look a thing like an iguanodon."

"The people who'd sponsored the reconstruction were so proud they all got together for a fancy dinner to celebrate the event—and the dinner was served to them *inside* one of the models," said Cobb with relish. "The guests included some of the most renowned gentlemen of Victorian natural philosophy. Including Professor Owen, after whom we've named the mountain."

"Charles Darwin too?" Holder asked, though he knew better.

"Oh no. This was years before the *Origin,* and Darwin and Owen became bitter enemies anyway. Very ironic in retrospect, but Owen, who coined the word *dinosaur,* would have absolutely nothing to do with the notion of evolution. He did his best to sink Darwin."

"But what about *your* iguanodon?" Alex prompted.

"Oh yes," said Cobb. "Well, we've reconstructed Mr. Hawkins's model and set it aside as a sort of private dining room. It seats three or four people quite comfortably. How they ever got twenty or more in *their* model, I'll never know."

Holder grinned his appreciation. "I look forward to the experience, Mr. Cobb."

Cobb nodded, pleased that the Chief Ranger had given him

the opportunity to trot out this well-polished anecdote. "Very nice to meet you, Mr. Unwin. See you gentlemen later this evening." He walked away.

Alex turned back to Frank Seaton, looking at him thoughtfully. He knew, as did Philip Holder, that Seaton didn't make casual remarks. He'd brought up the episode of the rescued tyrannosaur for a reason.

Holder still clearly recalled one of Seaton's finer moments, when the wiry black little man had been cursing and spitting and holding on to the tail of a peckerish juvenile rex for dear life, as he wrestled it back into the stockades away from the tops pens. One whiff of rex could turn a placid triceratops cow into a 8,000-kilogram battering ram that no fence could restrain. Seaton wasn't so much bothered by the struggle the little dickens was putting up (after all, it was hardly more than a baby, not even two meters long); it was the foul-smelling tyrannosaur shit he was getting all over his new high-heeled boots and twill trousers.

Holder treasured his memories of Seaton, who had taught him never to fear animals, but to treat them with precisely the respect they deserved. Cowardice and courage were inconsequential concepts in Seaton's view of the world; informed action was everything.

"Frank, we're wasting too much time and energy pulling gorgos and rexes out of the swamp these days. Animals that should be surviving on their own," said Alex.

"Might think about higher ground," said Seaton.

"Okay, I'm thinking."

"A rex's just like any other carnivore, Alex—just plays the odds. Rather eat fresh dead meat than alive. Failing that, rather catch 'em old or sick. I've seen a few rexes in hot pursuit go after prey in deep water, but they won't do that if they have a choice."

"They do a lot better down south of the river," Alex said. "Away from the tourists. They might do better yet inland."

"Might," Seaton agreed. He'd made his point.

Alex looked at Holder. "Sorry to bore you with all this shop talk, Mr. Unwin."

"Oh, that's fine with me," said Holder. "I'm fascinated." And he was; he'd never been included in these discussions when he'd been a boy.

"Sure," Alex grunted. "Hope you still think so a year from now. You and I got anything left to settle?"

Holder spoke cautiously. "You're offering me the job?"

"Already did. You're qualified, and I like your looks—a lot better than I thought I would, to tell the truth. I think the salary's fair, so now I'd say it's up to you. Can you take a couple of years in the wilderness surrounded by primitive brutes—such as me and Seaton here?"

Holder laughed. "I believe the answer is yes, Ranger."

"Alex. Here's to you, Telly-whatever. How the hell do you pronounce that? Now you work for me I can't go around calling you by your last name all the time."

"Just call me T.T. It's simpler." Holder raised his glass. "To you, Alex. And you, Frank."

"To a bright future, T.T." said Alex.

Holder's future as T.T. almost ended abruptly.

The three men set off early the next morning for the wharf, descending Waterhouse's main staircase to ground level and letting themselves through the electrified steel gate. Alex's limp was pronounced this early in the day, though he would lose it as he warmed up. Despite his wife's urgings, he'd never had his leg properly regenerated after his brush with a gorgo some years earlier. Holder suspected he was proud of the stigma.

The morning was fragrant with the perfume of magnolias, softened by the calls of primitive water birds. In the ponds the sauropods browsed. To Holder they were a familiar and comforting sight, a sign of home. He had grown up with dinosaurs as few others had, and in fact was more comfortable around them than his father was. Dinosaurs had been Philip Holder's pets, beasts of burden, and occasionally the brute adversaries against which he'd pitted his emerging manhood.

Waterhouse was built well above ground—a tyrannosaur could just stand erect beneath the floor of the elevated buildings. In an effort to create a sense of wild country the kilometer-long path from the dock was at ground level, carried on wooden causeways over the surface of the ponds for most of the distance. With nothing between the walkway and the water but a wooden handrail, the naive tourist got a thrilling (in fact, somewhat frightening) sense of exposure, for semi-aquatic sauropods, wholly peaceable creatures, often waded within touching distance.

Here and there the path crossed potentially dangerous firm ground. If a tourist were to find himself trapped in a milling herd of hadrosaurs he might soon be trampled all innocently into the gooey mud. Herbivorous dinosaurs had no fear of humans, nor any real consciousness of humans at all, and would step on a man as casually as on a beetle. Therefore over dry land the path was lined with barrier fences, picturesquely overgrown with lianas and flowering creepers, but constructed of polysteel posts sunk in concrete.

The men were halfway to the river on a stretch of path bordered by the tall barriers when an enormous adult rex stepped right through the fence in front of them. It was not chasing anything. Apparently it had merely blundered into the fence, by chance stumbling into a section whose foundations had been invisibly undermined. The rex blinked its red eyes. Only a moment passed before the giant reptile realized its good fortune.

"The water, Frank!" Alex bellowed. He was several steps in front of the others, nearest the animal. He turned to run.

The tyrannosaur took one tentative step. Then another. And suddenly the ground trembled under the beast's awesome charge. A deep and horrifying roar blasted from its throat.

The protective fence now prevented escape. It was twenty meters back along the path to the nearest open water. Momentarily Alex considered the fence itself—easy enough to climb if there were time, but he would be nowhere near the top before the rex was on him.

Frank Seaton was already running away as fast as his legs would carry him, screaming at the top of his lungs and waving his arms wildly. His behavior was a parody of stark terror, a calculated attempt to draw the animal's attention.

The Chief Ranger stood immobile. He had not panicked; there was simply nothing to be done. He could not climb fast enough, and even with two perfectly good legs he could not have outrun a tyrannosaur. He turned to face the beast, determined to look his death in the eye.

Tyrannosaurus rex presents two major problems to an adversary, one at each end: a mouthful of grisly teeth and a skull-cracking tail. Its tiny forelegs are so short they are useless in an argument, and the beast is so ponderous that, unlike its much smaller and more agile predecessor *Deinonychus* ("terrible claw"), it cannot stand on one hind leg while slashing out with the other. The safest place to be in the immediate vicinity of a hungry rex is underneath it.

The creature's jaws were wide and already swooping down when Holder hit the Chief Ranger from behind and took him to earth in a flying tackle. The blow was so strong that the men fell in a heap together, Holder on top.

The rex had a choice: it could back up a step and look for the morsels that had but lately been right before it, or it could go after Seaton, who was in plain view and behaving the way ordinary carnosaur prey *should* behave.

The two Holders lay panting on the ground beneath twin columns of muscle and bone and gristle that supported the monster's improbable bulk, waiting for its tiny brain to grind out a decision. The three-toed, meter-wide claw beside them lifted from the mud. . . .

A rex always plays the odds, Seaton had said, and so it was: the dinosaur took off in pursuit of Frank Seaton. Since a running theropod carries its tail high, the Holders escaped unscathed.

Phil Holder scrambled to his feet and gave his father a hand up. They ducked through the gap the rex had made in the fence. Seaton had already made good his escape, diving into the water several meters ahead of the rex.

"Hope that animal doesn't follow him in," the Ranger gasped. "We'll have the devil's own time getting it out."

"People are coming from the hotel," Holder said.

"Curare guns. Knock him out. Nothing short of a rocket will kill him, and when they see we're safe they won't do that."

They heard splashing in the water, and saw Frank Seaton swim toward them and drag himself out onto the muddy shore. He was breathing hard. He turned to watch the action behind them, toward the hotel.

They could all see the rex's head above the fence, searching in frustration. They saw men and women from the hotel pounding across the wooden bridge toward the dinosaur. The tyrannosaur roared defiance and stood its ground. A man raised a heavy rifle to his shoulder and fired. The tyrannosaur screamed and suddenly sat down out of sight behind the fence. The barrier sagged with its weight.

"Good shot!" said Alex with satisfaction. "Didn't topple him over and break his damn fool neck."

Only then did Holder reflect how the real T.T. Unwin would have behaved in this spot. The authentic Unwin had once distinguished himself by running in terror from the camp's mascot, a toothless egg-stealer that had approached him for a handout. The mooching oviraptor was the same size as a plucked turkey, and looked rather like one.

Holder put the thought out of his mind. This was a different world, and he hoped to make it even more different yet.

Holder noticed that the dripping-wet Seaton's attention had shifted from the dinosaur to him. He swallowed. "Lucky, weren't we?"

Seaton said nothing. Holder knew Frank Seaton didn't believe in luck.

14

Claymore sent helot guards for Unwin, but she went after Sirich herself.

"I've never been kidnapped so politely," said Sirich. "I don't suppose you would allow me to contact an attorney? I'll be sure to make a point of your good manners."

Claymore smiled and shook her head.

"Well, consider this an official protest, then." The old woman's face crinkled in amusement. "Though to tell the truth, I'm rather enjoying the change of pace."

Since the previous day when Bicknell at Security Headquarters had confirmed that Claymore would be assigned a Sprint, Unwin and Sirich had worked full time deriving the transfer values. Strangely, Sirich and Claymore had conceived a liking for each other within that brief time span. At first Claymore thought it was routine, one-way, induced trust, which Claymore had used on both Sirich and Unwin for simple insurance. While that might account for Sirich's friendliness, it would not account for Claymore's liking of Sirich—who had induced what in whom?

Moving stairs sped them toward the roof. They left behind thousands of people moving quietly along the softly lit vine-draped tiers of the building's vast internal cavity, people on the way to home or work or wherever their errands took them during the soleri's never ending cycle of activity. Claymore and Sirich observed the convention of silence until the escalator carried them past the top stratum of the mountainous structure. Then Claymore said, "Do you see why I won't believe the horrible odds you and Unwin are projecting?"

"I think the next few days will be interesting, Angelica, but I also suspect they will be my last," Sirich replied soberly. "I'm a very old woman. The prospect of death neither entices nor terrifies me."

They came to the traffic control barrier. An armed helot guard watched from the sentry post, impassive and immobile. Claymore held her thumb against the sensor plate. "Claymore," she told the guard. "Accompanied by Clarissa Sirich. Authorized." The barrier slid away and both women passed through.

Through the curve of the glass roof they could see Claymore's airplane on the pad a few meters away, waiting to take them into the low orbit where the Sprint was parked. The plane's black skin reflected dull red rhythmic flashes from the soleri's overhead aircraft warning beacons. The launch deck was narrow; beyond the edge of the finger-like concrete projection was a hazy night sky and nothing else.

"Unwin's behind schedule," said Claymore. "The security here is lax."

"One of San Francisco's traditional attractions," Sirich remarked.

"We'll wait here a moment." Claymore looked at Sirich curiously. "If you and Unwin are so pessimistic, why did you cooperate with Philip Holder?"

"You're a perceptive woman. Surely it's plain to you—Unwin's jocund exterior notwithstanding—that he hates Holder's memory?"

The thought had not occurred to Claymore.

"I'm sure that's why he cheerfully assisted in what he was certain would be Holder's doom," Sirich continued. "Even to providing him with old moneyslivers and other bits of identification, and helpful hints on what to do when he arrived on Darwin. I wouldn't be surprised if some of that information was deliberately phony—just in case Phil *did* get through."

"Unwin does seem to want to hedge his bets. And you, Clarissa? Why did you help Holder? Didn't you share Unwin's hopes for the outcome?"

"I'm an old spinster—perhaps I let Phil's handsome charm

carry me away." Sirich grinned impishly. "That's Unwin's interpretation. But the truth is, at first I thought I was just helping him pursue an intellectual curiosity. Later he convinced me he knew what he was doing, and had every right to do it. Conversely, I had no right to stand in his way."

"Even if you thought he'd kill himself?" Claymore's voice conveyed the inborn fear and disgust of any native of Earth for any instance of avoidable, irreversible death.

"The same probabilities that dictated death for most Phil Holders, most of his Doppelgängers, assured me that some at least would survive. An extraordinary moral dilemma," Sirich said as an afterthought, as if commenting on a particularly challenging math problem.

Now they spotted Unwin arriving at the top of the last escalator, far off among the shadows under the domed roof. He was closely escorted by gray-uniformed helots, one at each elbow. His step was heavy and slow.

The two women watched a moment in silence. Then Claymore said, "You claim that most of the Philip Holders *did* die . . ." She shuddered. "I don't know what I'm saying when I say that. It sounds preposterous."

"Yes, I'm sure most Phil Holders did die, Angelica. So will most of us—most yous, most mes, most Unwins. Painlessly, of course."

"What of the other obvious interpretation, Clarissa? That there's no record of Holder's success because *we* have already prevented it."

"Have it your way." Sirich shrugged. "Unwin and I are giving you the best calculations we can, to help you follow Phil. Still, I think our chances of personal survival, in the words of the old saying, are those of a snowflake in hell."

Unwin and his escorts approached the barrier. Through the clear barrier Claymore could see that Unwin was extremely agitated. His face was flushed, and he would not look at either woman.

"He's going to need sedation," said Claymore, annoyed. For a moment she wondered if Sirich and Unwin weren't mounting some elaborate charade. She didn't want to believe it of Sirich, but she wasn't sure she could trust her own feelings.

An instant later the question was tabled. As the barrier parted in front of Unwin, he took advantage of a moment's freedom to bolt for the doors that opened onto the landing pad.

The guards and the sentry fumbled for their sidearms simultaneously, like synchronized automata.

"No!" Claymore ordered. "Leave this to me!"

Two of the helots obeyed her immediately, standing aside, but the third, one of Unwin's escorts, paid no attention to her, apparently confused. He raised his weapon and took aim.

As Claymore moved for the guard she noticed something odd from the corner of her eye: Unwin had paused well within range, frozen in anticipation of the helot's next move.

A firegun is a terrifying psychological weapon, but rarely lethal unless the victim invites it. Claymore brushed the helot's hand aside just as he squeezed off a bolt. The blob of fire blackened the glass beside Unwin's head. By now Claymore had the guard's hand between her thumb and fingers.

The weapon clattered to the floor. The man's face twisted in reflexive pain and he turned toward her, wildly swinging his other hand. She stepped aside, planted her feet well apart, and with a graceful flowing downward motion of her arm and shoulder assisted the helot into a spectacular somersault; he landed in a heap two meters away.

Clearly someone had been tampering with the helot.

By the time Claymore's attention was once more focused on Unwin the stout old man had turned and begun to run, throwing aside the outer doors and dashing onto the landing pad. Claymore hesitated. If he were headed for the plane she would have to draw her own weapon and drop him before he could damage it.

But he ran past it, right to the edge of the pad. And he ran over the edge without hesitation . . .

He would not stop falling for half a thousand meters. The velocity with which he struck the ground would be only somewhat moderated by wind resistance.

Claymore stared after him in horror. Trembling, she turned to Sirich, who stood bright-eyed and alert beside the barrier. "What was that?" Claymore demanded hoarsely. "Are you all in some mad league of suicides?"

The old woman's voice was sharp. "Welcome to the club."

15

The buzzing airboat skidded around a bend in the broad river. Ahead lay the Administrative Headquarters for Upper and Lower Cretacia, less formally known as Camp Owen Gorge.

The Camp was a tiny place, even allowing for Holder's exaggerated childhood memories. In all Cretacia, half a Darwinian continent, there were no more than ten thousand legal residents, most of them living in Copeville, where they were directly engaged in the tourist trade. Cretacia belonged to the dinosaurs.

From the Camp broad lawns descended to the river. The Chief Ranger's quarters stood at the top of a grassy rise under big old shade trees, the largest of a series of connected dormitories and staff apartments, low earth-colored buildings with roofs of dark red tile. Hidden behind the living quarters, Holder knew, were laboratories extending several hectares back into the jungle. Though not the great basic research establishment to be found at the Institute in Cuvier, these practical field facilities could nevertheless make *ad hoc* repairs to an organism, collect and record data, and, when necessary, grow a good-sized animal from scratch.

Downriver were pens for animals not yet released into the wild, or temporarily withdrawn from the struggle for existence. The immense saurian feedlot was partially hidden behind thick stands of monkey puzzle, but its penetrating odor, not unlike that of a pig farm, was undisguisable. Holder would have to get used to it all over again.

Just upriver rose reddish-black cliffs lushly overgrown with ferns, the first of a series of huge stairsteps building up to the smooth slopes of Owen. Here the muddy waters of the Marsh descended in mighty cataracts over colossal piles of basalt thrown down from the heights in the geologically recent past. Beyond this point no human could penetrate Cretacia except on the back of an animal or in an aircraft. The clattering roar of a huge waterfall issued from the great fissure in the cliffs, as if from a megaphone.

"Noisy out here on the river," Alex shouted at Holder, "but once we get in the shadow of the cliffs it's not that bad."

As he spoke the speeding boat passed into the shelter of the cliff. The roar subsided. A cool spray of water soothed Holder's overloaded senses with a dank perfume of mud and fish and algae.

"Couple of hundred years ago, at the time of the Reformation, there was a big soleri across the mouth of this canyon," Alex said. "Produced hydro power, housed maybe 20,000. Ripped it all out. Hardly recognize the ruins, now."

Frank Seaton expertly piloted the pontooned boat toward the docks, cutting propellor power at the last moment. A whiff of ozone and hot lubricant overtook Holder as the boat slowed. The twin hulls settled deeply into the opaque green water, and the boat drifted to a stop beside the wharf.

Seaton was quickly over the side onto the boards of the wharf, taking turns of the painter around an iron cleat. Holder clambered onto the dock and turned to give Alex a hand with the bags, but Alex was already ashore. He handed Holder his canvas satchel, and spoke to Seaton. "Thanks, Frank. Give me a report when the copter crew gets back, will you? I want to know the rex is all right and the fence is back together. I won't clear the *Marsh Queen* until I hear that."

"Sure thing, Alex."

"One more thing. Let's move fast on your idea of moving more theropods inland. Starting with that big dumb one who attacked us. Will you plot the logistics on that?"

"No problem, Alex." Seaton jumped back into the boat, securing its tackle.

"Meet with you tomorrow morning." Alex turned to Holder. "Let's go. I'll introduce you to Phil and show you around."

They turned toward shore. A teen-aged boy had run down to the dock to meet them, a skinny kid with huge feet and a big-eyed, oddly lopsided face. His skin, the more or less standard human-colored skin of all the non-Earth worlds, was even more darkly bronzed by constant exposure to tropical sunlight, and he had a sprinkle of mahogany freckles across the bridge of his short nose. For just the barest instant Holder wondered whose he was.

"Hi, Phil," said Alex. "Where's Mom?"

The boy shrugged, adolescent sign language for "How should *I* know?"

Holder stared at him. Oddly, he felt nothing for the moment beyond intellectual curiosity. No wonder the face looked lopsided: it was mirror reversed. Himself. He hadn't recognized himself.

For his part young Phil seemed mildly curious about Holder, but too defiantly shy to stare at him.

"Son, this is Mr. T.T. Unwin, the teacher we talked about." Alex smiled. "I'll let him tell you what the T's are for."

Phil glared at Holder then, but still he made no move.

"Shake hands like a man, Phil," his father said impatiently.

Phil lurched forward and held out a paw that was as enormous, proportionally, as his feet. "Nice to meet you, Mr. Unwin," he muttered almost inaudibly.

"Call me T.T.," said Holder heartily. He took the boy's hand and his skin prickled, his stomach fluttered. He forced himself to endure it. The sensation was distinctly odd, like nothing he'd experienced except for a few times when he'd caught a whiff of a baby's milky breath—and when he'd tried to report the strange queasiness of that experience to others, seeking confirmation, no one had known what he was talking about; he'd hypothesized sensitivity to some particular organic molecule and let it go at that.

Phil pulled his hand away from Holder's.

"Good to meet you, Phil," said Holder hastily, realizing he'd been clinging to the boy's hand overlong. "You're bigger than I expected." (Damn! What a stupid thing to say—of all people, *I* should know how sensitive he is.)

"Fresh air's good for him," Alex said with satisfaction. "Phil, take T.T.'s bag. We'll go up to the house and find the miz."

"I can handle it," said Holder as Phil reached for his overnight bag.

Phil gave him a reproachful look. His father had told *him* to take the bag; the matter was not for argument. Holder dropped it like a hot potato.

They set off across the lawn, Alex marching ahead, Phil hurrying to catch up to his side, Holder bringing up the rear. He had not made an auspicious introduction to himself.

"Did you fight a big rex, Dad?" Phil asked his father breathlessly. "They said on the radio . . ."

"Yeah, it was interesting for a minute. Actually T.T. here

saved the day." Alex laughed. "And he's never seen a dinosaur up close! Maybe he didn't know enough to be scared, eh, T.T.?"

"It wasn't really . . ." Holder began, before he realized Phil was ignoring him.

"What'd you do, roll under him?" Phil asked his father.

"That's how we ended up."

"Yeah, that's just what I would have done," said Phil, boasting wistfully.

Holder heard the aching love in the boy's voice as Phil attempted to identify with his father's tribulations, heard it expressed as an assumed sophistication about the ways of dinosaurs and Rangers. And Alex was sending signals just as false, in attempting to downplay his danger. Holder was helpless to clear up the miscommunication. The shadings of meaning were so delicate, and so delicately misconstrued, that any attempt to clarify them would make them worse. Some aspects of adolescence were going to have to run their course without his interference.

Lost in these reveries Holder almost collided with Alex, who had stopped on the porch of the big house. Phil went inside first, pushing the wide wooden door aside, shouting, "Mom? You in here? Dad's home."

Holder followed Alex into the cool dark house. He smelled a peculiar odor, a pleasant odor, compounded of just what he was not sure. There was furniture polish and dust in the drapes and a whiff of musty fungus, a woman's perfume and a residual tobacco smell from Alex's occasional pipe, and some originally vile-scented spray meant to keep all these other smells at bay (it had lost the battle). It was the quintessential smell of home; no holo, no souvenir, not even living, breathing people out of his past had convinced Holder so surely as this faint aroma that he was really *here*.

He glanced to his left, into the darkened living room with its grey rugs, its book-lined shelves, its tasteful scenic oils, its perhaps too overly refined overstuffed chairs and couch. All was there, just where it should be.

He glanced back, eager to peer into the other rooms of the house. A woman was standing in front of him.

(Be honest. She's not *that* beautiful . . .)

"Mr. Unwin? I'm Isabel Holder. I'm pleased to see you."

Isabel Holder was shorter than Alex, but seemed taller. To Holder she seemed tall, cool, elegant—utterly inviting and utterly unapproachable. Forced to be rational, he would have described her as a well-bred, withdrawn, generally pleasant brunette woman of about thirty-five, but at the moment he was incapable of any such clear-eyed description.

Already she had moved to place herself between "Unwin" and her son Phil. Perfectly conscious that her husband had hired Unwin to take charge of her child, she was prepared to dislike him intensely. Her resentment was not lost on Holder. Presumably poor Unwin—the real Unwin—had experienced the same hostility; he'd had no choice but to stick it out, and neither did Holder. Holder felt distinctly unwelcome in what was after all his own family home.

"You'll want to rest and freshen up, Mr. Unwin," said Isabel. "Join us in an hour for lunch." She turned to her husband. "You'll have lunch at home today, won't you, Alex? Surely you've done enough work for one day."

"Oh, sure, dear. You heard about the . . ."

"Yes," she said firmly, in a tone indicating she didn't want to discuss it front of Phil.

Alex turned to Phil. "Show T.T. to his room, son. You know the one. We'll see you in about an hour, I guess, T.T."

"Fine, Alex. Until later, Mrs. Holder."

Phil led Holder through the shadowy cool lanai onto the flagstone path behind the house. The path ran under a low arcade, wooden beams with a tiled roof overgrown with flowering vines. The arcade connected all the living quarters, winding through an arboretum of exotic trees and shrubs and ferns.

Unwin's quarters were in the low building that contained apartments for single lab workers. Phil set Holder's satchel down inside the door. He remained standing outside when Holder walked in. "See you later, Mr. Unwin," he said, taking a backward step.

"Wait, Phil," Holder said quickly. "Have you got anything planned for this afternoon? I could use a tour."

"Sure, I guess. I didn't have anything special planned."

"Look, call me T.T., okay? I'm not used to being a 'Mister.' "

Phil shrugged, adolescent for "Whatever you want."

Holder stood speechless. For the life of him he could think of nothing to keep the conversation going. "Okay. See you later. Thanks."

Phil fled instantly. Holder watched him running away, feet

and elbows flying, back to the house. Holder, alone in the little room that he already knew so well, felt like an interloper in territory that rightfully belonged to the eagerly departed Unwin. He unzipped his bag and took out the few clothes it contained. There were hangers in the single closet. In a few moments he had put away everything he owned.

He sat down on the folding bed and stared at the wall. Maybe he'd take a shower in a minute. There was lots of time to kill. There would be lots more time to kill, in the future.

16

> "Welcome to Darwin! Whether this is your first visit or your hundred–and–first, we want you to have an enjoyable stay. . . .
>
> . . .
>
> "You may have heard rumors about Darwin's Uniform Code of Natural Human Life—there certainly have been some tall tales! So let's make it clear right now, we *don't* deport twins! But seriously—the only thing you need to remember about the Uniform Code is that it applies only to permanent residents. We respect the customs of your home just as we expect you to respect ours. We're not prejudiced—if you're a clone, even if you're a mosaic!—whoever you are, whatever you are, if you're a *visitor*, you are Welcome to Darwin!"
>
> (from *Welcome to Darwin,* a publication of the Darwin Visitors Bureau)

Almost a month after Holder reached Camp Owen Gorge the robot monitors orbiting Darwin Station detected an unidentified, unannounced ship emerging at well over a third of light speed. The monitors flashed an alert to Traffic Control. Traffic Control would do its best to intercept, but, as frequently happened, it would fail. Customs officers would attribute failure to the superb equipment carried by smugglers; the high price of contraband made a large capital investment in evasion gear affordable and worthwhile.

Customs could not know that the invader's equipment was so advanced no money of the time could have bought it. The Earth ship was Sprint class, Security's fastest and most sophisticated recon and infiltration classification, with the advantage of thirty years' technical refinement.

"Darwin's Star," Claymore said. She was relieved, and she felt a bit smug. "Despite all your fears, we made it." She switched the control computer to deceleration sequence. The freely falling ship began to wheel slowly in space.

Sirich watched the drifting stars through the unshielded windows. She smiled faintly. "I wonder if we were the only ones?"

Claymore brushed *auburn hair from her hazel eyes*. "That hardly matters, Clarissa." *One might still compare the heart-shaped face of this Claymore Doppelgänger to that of the Mona Lisa—for on the Earth she'd just come from Leonardo had painted a woman with auburn hair.*

"You're right," the Sirich Doppel said. "The only reality that concerns us is the one where we are."

The main engine fired and the ship began its long descent. Almost as an afterthought, Angelica Claymore reset the clock.

Stage Two: Darwin, 176 N.E.

17

Kani paused, motionless on the sun-dappled ridgetop path, lifting his golden head higher in the fragrant air. He sniffed. Amid the perfumes of the pines and grasses and wildflowers he noted the peculiar musky-dry odor of triceratops.

He moved along the path, seeking an opening in the close ranks of pine and juniper. At a bend in the trail the trunks thinned. Below, the narrow canyon wound toward the great Gorge of the River, while behind him, hidden by dark branches overhead, the slopes of the Mountain of Vapors rose gradually for many miles into the realm of the sky demons.

A gust of wind blew up the canyon, quivering the ruffled leaves of the gingko trees. With it came olfactory evidence of at least a dozen of the big herbivorous dinosaurs, not far off—and of something else as well. Kani wrinkled his nose. In this heat it didn't take a sensitive nose to identify the stink of a crowd of sweaty humans.

He stared for a moment at the small sun-dried red clay statuette he carried in his right hand, a crude representation of a tyrannosaur. He was taking it to the Shrine of the Spring, a day's journey from the village, partly to ask the help of the Goddess, partly to be away from the village on the day of the Trader's annual visit. He had contributed nothing to the piles of colorful hides the adult hunters would offer, and he could not endure their mockery. No one in the village had seen a real tyrannosaur within living memory, but Kani thought that if he were going to offer only a model he, the least of men, might as well offer the greatest of creatures.

He placed the figurine in the crook of a shaggy juniper. Unencumbered now by any implement except the long coil of grass rope that hung from his shoulder, nor by any scrap of clothing except a twist of string around his loins—and of course his necklace of trade teeth, the badge of an initiate—

he left the trail and began working his way down the slope through a thick tangle of brush.

Skirting an impenetrable thicket of oleander, he darted through a grove of ginkgos, his golden skin and hair blending so well with the shimmering light from the green-gold trees that if he had merely stood still he would have become instantly invisible to any watcher.

Now he could hear the rush of water over rocks, and over that sound an occasional whistle or shout, which fired his curiosity. He could see nothing but a glittering mosaic of translucent leaves. Even underfoot the fallen leaves were thick, cushioning the tread of his bare feet.

Abruptly the slope became steeper, falling off sharply in a treacherous slide of wet leaves and slick red mud. The stream was loud now, and the air was cool with spray, and still he could see nothing. Cautiously he crept along the bank, screened from the invisible rushing river by a tangle of wild fig branches.

He came to an immense lava boulder thrusting up through the net of leaves and branches. The rock's steep, faceted sides were thickly upholstered with bright green moss—his fingers and toes wriggled for holds in the treacherous matting as he pulled himself to the top. He emerged into sunlight, suddenly conscious of his bright conspicuous hair. Flat on his stomach he wormed forward to the edge and peered over.

What he saw stunned him.

A line of great leathery creatures splashed upstream over the rounded boulders of the river. Many had already passed and gone on upriver, and many more still approached, ponderous but unimpeded. Their tiny amber eyes shone dully in their massive beaked heads, which were imperially crested and horned with long pikes of bone. Long hind legs and short forelegs propelled them forward, sure-footed but rhythmically lurching.

Kani had seen families of triceratops before, whole herds moving in habitual single file as these creatures did. What made him stare in fear and astonishment were the riders. On each broad back where it sloped sharply down from elevated hips rode a man or woman, swaying to and fro in a nest of boxes and bundles. He knew them immediately by their uniforms of green and brown, and by their black skin: Rangers.

Kani had thought Rangers were merely the exaggerated villains of old husbands' tales, evil bugaboos useful for scaring bold children. Occasionally the old folks would point to a sky machine passing high overhead and identify it by its spinning wings as a Ranger's. Yet here were men and women riding on the backs of dinosaurs, an occult power possessed only by demons of the dark forest and the mountain mists—or by Rangers.

Kani watched fascinated, scarcely daring to breathe, as the colossal caravan stumbled to a halt. Just below his eyrie an animal stood stolidly in midstream, waiting, while the animals in the lead left the river bank and, urged on by their riders, began clearing a path up the far slope of the canyon. Their long horns rooted out bushes and tossed them aside. Clouds of dust and insects rose around the riders, who constantly whistled and clucked. The triceratops moved mechanically ahead. Kani could see that an hour or so of such work would succeed in beating a broad trail up to the open pine woods on top of the opposite ridge, the edge of a broad plateau. The dinosaur riders were heading into the black forests west of the great Gorge, where even the people themselves rarely wandered. What could Rangers want so deep in the people's country?

Kani studied the pair nearest him, an old man of perhaps forty seasons, and a soft-looking youth, both perched on the back of the triceratops that had stopped below his rock. They certainly looked human enough, except for their black skins. They were gabbling Ranger talk to each other, and Kani strained to hear what this exotic speech might sound like.

His skin prickled. Had serpents licked his ears in the night? It was the same as the people's speech. He could *understand what the Rangers were saying.*

The night approach terrified Claymore, despite her faith in the Sprint and its programmed landing instructions. Outside the windows jagged pinnacles slid past, shifting in the light of the racing moon. Then the slender ship slowed, to thread its way between desolate scarps toward a glacier-hung cirque. Supported on nearly invisible columns of blue flame, the Sprint lowered itself onto, and then into, the ice. They had landed only forty kilometers from Cuvier, but they were several thousand meters up in the rugged Lyell Range.

In the dim green glow of the cramped cabin Claymore stripped and began pulling a thermal suit over her long, bare limps. The suit looked no more complicated or elegant than old-fashioned long johns, but it was all she needed to survive the freezing journey ahead.

Sirich watched from her couch. "I suppose it's into the deepfreeze for me?" she remarked in resignation.

Claymore smiled. "We've been over this, Clarissa. I just can't justify taking you. I'll leave you a wake-up call in case something happens to me."

"I have no motive for helping Phil any further, Angelica, especially since you assure me you mean him no harm. And I could be useful."

"Clarissa . . ." Claymore had to break off as she pulled the upper half of the suit over her head.

Sirich took advantage of the other woman's momentary helplessness to press her case: "I've been to Darwin, I know the administrative procedures. You know I can manipulate a computer—in case there's a problem with your forgeries. It *is* thirty years earlier, you know. Before your time."

Claymore settled the suit under her breasts and sealed the waist seam. "Thirty years less a month," she reminded Sirich. "Maybe you've already helped Holder to a head start."

"One month in thirty years is less than three-tenths of a percent error with an experimental technique. We don't even know Holder's gotten here yet himself! Or maybe he's been here a year already. You're unfair. And besides . . ."

Claymore went about packing, listening to her friend's arguments repeated for the third or fourth time. Nothing Sirich said was new, nothing was compellingly persuasive—yet now there was some indefinable element: the calm, insightful manner, perhaps, the words that came just so, in response to thoughts Claymore had not yet spoken, or the undercurrent of trust, of love . . . With astonishment Claymore realized she was changing her mind.

18

Fingernails scratched at the door post. "Come in, Meria," said the Mother.

The priestess Meria pushed aside the curtain of pebbled

crocodile leather and stepped into the Mother's house. "He's almost here, Ariana," the tall blonde priestess said. "One of the men saw his sky machine circling against the dawn."

"Help me with this, Meria." The Mother Ariana turned so that Meria could reach the clasps of the heavy choker that lay over her breasts; it was a massive piece, constructed of ankylosaur bone plates studded with beaten river gold. "This old thing is not only ugly, it's impossible to put on."

"This is the symbol of your power, Mother," said Meria, faintly scandalized, though by now she should have been accustomed to Ariana's bluntness. She tied the choker's thongs, then stepped around to check Ariana's coiffure and her palm fiber skirt, as golden as her hair. "You are fit to receive the Trader now, Ariana," Meria said with satisfaction.

"How gratifying. I wish he were fit to receive me," Ariana said sourly.

Meria kept a politic silence; she fussed with the food and drink laid out on the trestle table, the smoked fish and the fresh figs, the deviled lizards' eggs, the turtle meat, the wine, the ama.

Ariana watched her a moment, then said impetuously, "Meria, I will not receive the Trader here. Offer him refreshment. When he has stuffed himself, bring him to me in the village shrine." Ariana left the surprised priestess standing by the table.

Outside her house the men were already gathering, chattering mindlessly as men do, resplendent in their capes of colored leather, their necklaces of teeth, their headdresses of painted bark sparkling with the bright green carapaces of tiny beetles. Stacked on each side of Ariana's woven-mat house were piles of crocodile skins, ankylosaur and scolosaur hides, triceratops horns, whole pteranodons stretched on wooden frames. The huge arch of the cave roof, the uncollapsed roof of the lava tube that sheltered the entire village, soared above the gay crowd.

The men grew silent as Ariana strode through their midst, toward the ravine. For the Mother to leave her house before the Trader arrived was a departure from tradition. They had no idea what to make of it.

She found the narrow path to the top of the deep ravine and soon left the puzzled villagers behind. She would start a new tradition today; she would receive the Trader in the shrine —not because of its beauty, still less because of its religious associations, but because of its acoustics. Voices from the ravine might float up to the shrine, but what she and the Trader said to each other on top of the cliffs would remain their own business. That she must deal with him at all galled her more with each season.

The symbiosis of Trader and people extended back beyond Ariana's ability to reckon. Farther back than her mother's mother (whom she could remember, but did not like) she knew only the names of ancestors, with no scrap of personal history to give them breath or business in the world.

Of course she knew the legends. They had been taught her not by her natural mother, but by Ariana her predecessor. Her real mother had died when she was eight or nine, her father a year later.

The people pitied orphans but did not value them. A girl without parents could not pay a groom price, and she was regarded with open suspicion by the mothers of eligible young men, who naturally hoped to make the most advantageous matches possible for their sons. Vera—Ariana's given name—drifted from relative to relative, learning to keep her mouth shut and her eyes and ears open. An outsider in her own community, she thought much on the customs of the people, and decided that not everything she saw was self-evidently wise and good.

Vera was fifteen when the natural Successor, a girl her own age, died of disease. She was as startled as everyone else when, after a suitable period of mourning, the old Mother Ariana claimed that the Goddess had appeared in a dream and commanded her to name Vera the new Ariana.

Then began the most intense year of her life, much of it spent beside the bed of the ailing Mother, wreathed in thick clouds of herbal smoke. All the while suppressing the urge to choke, she ingested what she could of the lore that was droned at her incessantly, night and day. She learned of the day when there were "cities" on Bounty—great piles of stone filled with people—and farms that stretched from horizon to horizon. In those days the ancestors of the people had not been farmers, for with machines to do the work there was no need. Instead the people had led a carefree life in the forest, selling sweet illicit herbs to their town cousins, who frowned on their way of life but bought their produce nevertheless. Then, surely, the people had all that the Goddess and life itself could have given them.

Then came the Death, and the Demons, and the Creatures of Darkness.

The new Ariana learned these stories well, but she learned more. She learned the old Ariana's doubts and opinions and plans. The old woman had truly mourned the loss of her daughter, but she had chosen the new Ariana with shrewd purpose, hoping through her to perpetuate her preparations for a day when the people could farm openly, and openly sell the produce of their gardens, and speak with their own voices in the councils of the world in which they lived.

And do away with the cynical criminals who dignified themselves with the title of Trader...

Ariana reached the top of the cliff and entered the shrine through the gap in the little withe fence. The sun was almost up now, and the sky beyond the shoulder of the mountain was brighter than the gold on her breast. Dark cypresses brooded over the shrine.

In the center of the uneven pavement of river pebbles stood a boulder of green jade, a pedestal for an awkward, tied-wicker contraption that only an initiate could have recognized as a model of the great robot plant processors that once prowled the wide plains of Bounty. The reliquary contained a bent and rusted scrap of iron said to have been, once upon a time, an actual part of just such a machine. Ariana seated herself on a bench in front of the quaint idol to wait for the Trader, the living symbol of the people's present predicament.

Evidently the Trader had decided to skip his breakfast, for only a few minutes passed before Meria appeared at the gate of the shrine, leading the visitor. Leaving him at the gate, Meria turned and quickly disappeared down the path. Ariana rose and took a step toward him, extending her right hand in the manner customary among outsiders. "How pleasant to see you again, Mr. Langoza," she said coolly.

Langoza stepped forward jauntily and took her hand, squeezing it a little too hard. "Delighted to see you looking so good, Mother."

Ariana thought perhaps he was not delighted. Perhaps he'd hoped to find her dead by now; she was over forty seasons, after all, and Langoza may have hoped to be dealing with her daughter, the Successor, who at sixteen was barely an adult.

Langoza was a contradictory fellow, conservative-looking if one went only by the dark face framed by neatly trimmed black beard and hair greying at the temples. But he was rakishly dressed in black boots and trousers, and he wore an open shirt of the softest yellow leather from the wings of a pteranodon. On his bared chest he sported a necklace of gorgosaur teeth, after the fashion of an Initiate. Ariana suspected he wore it to mock them.

She gestured at the bench. "Sit down, Trader. Tell me all your news. After I've heard what passes in the world outside we can relax with a pipe and a bowl, and I'll show you some trophies."

"Sounds great, Mother." He sprawled on the bench.

She sat facing him, as far away as she gracefully could manage.

Langoza assumed a sad look. "I'm afraid I got one big disappointment for you, Mother. You indicated to Mr. Wilson when he was up here last time that you desired to obtain certain specific drug items. I regret to tell you we just can't get 'em. We done our best, but these substances are controlled very rigorously here on Darwin—excuse, I mean Bounty—and on the other worlds, well, the demand . . ." He trailed off, as if unwilling to say what he meant, that Ariana's people could not possibly afford them.

The news hardly surprised her; indeed the story was always the same: modern medicines, modern tools, electronic devices for counting and time-keeping and for communicating across distances, somehow these things were never available, or only at exorbitant prices, in amounts so meager as to do nothing but whet the appetite. On the other hand . . .

"We got a terrific supply of cotton prints, some good iron knives, and a collection of beads that'll knock your eyes out," Langoza said with a broad grin. "And a very rare collection of teeth!" He waited for her exclamations of delight.

She looked at him without expression. Then she forced herself to smile as broadly as he. "The young men especially will be delighted to hear it, Trader. And what of the rest? Do you have needles, and fine, tough thread to go with your pretty cloth? Are your knives made of proper steel?—or are they like the last bunch, as rusted and soft as the heart of our venerable relic here?"

She listened to his ritual assurance of the quality of his goods with only half an ear. This stereotyped haggling wearied her unto death. In her own aching impatience she sensed the beginnings of change in the world, the coming of a time to throw caution and dissembling aside, along with all the dark old superstitious ways.

Langoza too seemed to sense something; his too-jovial manner betrayed his growing wariness of her. "Say, I almost forgot, Mother—and you asked for news of the outside!—I heard it on good authority those Rangers are bringing tyrannosaurs back to your neck of the woods. Won't *that* excite your young bucks!"

Ariana stared at him, jolted from her reveries. This news must not be spread through the village. She could imagine an orgy of frivolous young men rushing off, deserting their gardens, each eager to be the first to bring down the ancient prize. For Mother Bounty was said to love the blood of this beast above that of any other. Not to mention the Traders . . . "You must tell me more about this," she said as calmly as she could. "But privately. I don't want to unduly excite . . ."

"Sure, I can understand that," he said, blithely cutting her off. "Especially when they find out how much me and my associates are willing to pay for just one honest-to-God rex hide." Langoza laughed. "Hell, your boys would cut each other down to get first crack, won't they?"

She looked at him bitterly, recognizing the threat. "If the rumor is true, I will be happy to supply you with all the hides I can obtain. And since these hides are so valuable, you in turn will no doubt be able to locate a supply of the medicines we mentioned earlier."

He just kept grinning.

Ariana went on sternly. "But you must let me handle this my way, or there will be nothing for you. Nothing, do you understand?"

"There's other tribes," he said, his grin stiffening.

"Go to them with my blessing."

"Well, they ain't so advantageously situated as you people." He gave her a poisonous look. Then he shrugged. "Okay. I'll go along."

"Good. You see the matter as I do. We can proceed . . ." She smiled.

Kani entered the mouth of the ravine with automatic stealth, whistling the signal that warned the guards of his approach. The ravine had formed with the collapse of the huge lava tube centuries earlier; thick, rich soil had built up on its floor, supporting tall hardwoods draped with flowering vines, and spiny cycads and sturdy tree ferns—plus the people's most productive gardens.

As he moved into the green shadows under the trees he noted the Trader's big black sky machine parked just under the trees at the entrance to the ravine, its long wings folded into its sides.

The daughter-Ariana was sitting where Kani had hoped to find her, under a canopy of acacias near the mouth of the main cave. On the other side of the pool at the cave mouth the men of the tribe milled about in their finery. Ariana and her two half-sisters ignored them, concentrating on the long fibers they deftly twisted into rope. Ariana was making a lasso for her own use, while the efforts of her skinny sisters, still at the apprenticeship stage, would find some use in fence building or roof repair.

"Hello, Ariana," said Kani, trying to sound casual, though his chest was aching.

"Where are you going, Kani?" she asked quietly.

"To see your mother," he said. His fair skin burned with pride. "To discuss an offering."

Ariana gazed at him with pale blue eyes. Her sisters stopped their work. Maya, the older of the two, sniggered. Ariana looked down and resumed rolling and tugging the fiber cords between her strong fingers. "It will take more than the offer of a doll to interest my mother," she said, her voice hinting reproof. This time both Maya and her sister laughed, and Ariana silenced them with a stern glance.

"Though I have no house or garden yet, my offering will . . ." Kani stopped himself, then continued less pompously, "My offering will interest her, I'm sure."

"I pray that it does, Kani." She smiled at him wanly. "You will excuse us now, please. Apparently my infant siblings can not work and eavesdrop at the same time. Our mother's displeasure will be severe if they do not finish what they have started."

The little girls gave her withering sidelong glaces, but made no audible protest. Kani nodded at her, half raised his hand to say goodbye, and went on toward the main cave.

Beyond the deep blue-green pool at its entrance, the stone arch, hung with ferns, sheltered whole houses of woven mat and thatch. The gathered hunters ignored Kani as he pushed through them toward the Mother's house, the longest building in the cave. The priestess Meria and her brother Leri kept watch outside the Mother's door; the warrior priests were the Mother's prececessor's sisters' children, and held the guard duty by hereditary right. Kani went boldly up to the man.

"What do you want, Kani?" Leri asked lazily, not bothering to get up off his haunches. Leri was tough and scarred, at least thirty seasons old; his long yellow hair and beard were streaked with gray.

"I want to see the Mother. About an offering."

On the far side of the doorway Meria snorted, not bothering to hide her contempt.

"You were young once, I think," Leri said to his sister. He looked at Kani with sympathetic eyes, but he shook his head.

Kani flushed. "It is my right to see the Mother when . . ."

"Yes, yes. Not when she's with a Trader, though." Leri got to his feet, stiffly. "Take a walk with me, Kani." Before Kani could protest, Leri draped a heavily-muscled arm across the younger man's shoulders and drew him away, through the throng of jabbering men, toward the dark pool at the mouth of the cave. Across the clear, cold water Kani could see his beloved and her sisters, blazoned in filtered sunlight, working patiently.

Leri followed his gaze. "You're a lucky man, Kani," he said confidentally. "I think the Mother likes you well enough to give you a bit of time. And the little Mother will wait for you forever, by the look in her eye." Leri turned to face Kani. His bronzed face showed the deep creases of maturity, and he was not smiling. "So don't make a fool of yourself and lose your chance. Work. Gain a reputation. Build a house and prepare a plot—you've got to *prove* you're worth the groom price, man! Forget this talk of an offering until you have something the Goddess won't sneeze at."

"But I have, Leri, I have!" Kani said excitedly. "And I believe the Goddess herself has delivered the offering into my hands, for I was on the way to her with a doll of the tyrannosaur when . . ."

"What are you yammering about, boy?" Leri asked gruffly.

"The best offering of all, Leri. *Tyrannosaurus!* I know where to find one!"

Leri grabbed the younger man's jaw between horny thumb and fingers, effectively silencing him. He pulled Kani's face toward him, searching for signs of illness. Kani flinched, but stood rigid until the inspection was complete. Leri dropped his hand. "None have seen a living tyrannosaur in my lifetime. The Traders say they live only in the dawn lands, guarded by demon Rangers."

"But the Rangers are bringing them here! I've seen Rangers with my own eyes—yesterday. I heard them talking—I was no further from them than I am from the pool there, and I heard them tell how they will bring tyrannosaurs back to the deep forest."

"You heard them? You understood them?"

"They spoke the Speech, although so badly I wanted to laugh."

"When did this happen?" But Leri didn't wait for the answer. "No," he said. "It's not my place to hear this story, or to judge it. You wanted to see the Mother. Now you *must* see the Mother."

"Yes, he must," said Ariana's voice behind them.

They whirled to see the Mother herself standing a few feet away. Her aegis of gold and ivory glowed terribly in the cave's dim green light. Leri and Kani dropped to their knees and bowed their heads.

Behind her the other men of the tribe, bright as scraps of trade cloth, pressed forward, peering and straining to hear. Ariana turned to the dark Trader who stood beside her. "It seems your information was accurate, Mr. Langoza."

Langoza nodded smugly. "Ain't no secrets now, Mother."

"*I* choose who hunts *Tyrannosaurus*," she replied angrily. Her rich voice reverberated from the curved stone ceiling, and even Langoza flinched away from her. "No man will leave his gardens without my permission." The men muttered in dismay; she waited until the grumbling died, then looked at Langoza and at the kneeling Kani. "Both of you want the same thing for reasons of your own. Is it wise to let either of you have what you want?"

"Mother, you're wisdom incarnate," Langoza said, trying to be smooth, but managing only to sound frightened. "Whatever you decide."

"Come with me, Kani," she said with annoyance. "And you, Langoza. 'Wisdom incarnate' has questions for you both."

19

A stiff breeze whipped the blue-gray water to whitecaps. From the granite breakwater Angelica Claymore faced the fresh wind, filling her lungs with tangy air. Space! Everywhere she looked . . .

Gulls wheeled and screamed, and far out in the Kenyatta Inlet a sailboat beat upwind under close-hauled snapping canvas. The air was clear beneath gray clouds that jostled each other all the way to the horizon; across the inlet Claymore could see the granite cliffs of the Lyell Range rising up, sheer and grim, into the clouds.

The Esplanade that ringed Cuvier was bigger than the city itself; the park held at least one specimen of every tree and shrub and moss and flower that grew anywhere on the planet. Through the gardens wandered a collection of animals that would have confounded Noah.

Darwin's largest city was a village by Earth standards, with a resident population of some 200,000, and, on a typical day, half again as many tourists. Architecturally Cuvier was forgettable, a collection of practical polysteel and bright plastic boxes arranged on a simple grid plan. The important buildings, the Institute and the major hotels, were distinguished only by their rambling size. But the buildings were virtually invisible beneath a teeming reticulum of life, a profusion of fruiting and flowering, stickery-sticky, climbing, creeping, twisty-twining, budding and blooming vegetation. The birds and insects were almost as various, and if anything more numerous—so much underfoot and overhead that fastidious tourists complained. Claymore gloried in the hurlyburly; her heart lifted with every bird song, with each chitter and buzz and cluck of gecko or cricket or frog. She did not mistake diversity for freedom, but this tame nature seduced her.

Earth Security had supplied her with good programming data, or so it had seemed. She and Sirich had had no trouble getting rooms at the Burton, the city's largest hotel. They'd put in applications for travel permits on the basis of memberships in a big tour from Earth, and had expected routine overnight approval. This morning they should have been on their way to Copeville aboard the daily airship.

Their room terminal had politely informed them of a temporary processing delay, and had reminded them that they were not to venture outside the limits of Cuvier until their permits had been approved.

Sirich had volunteered to check into the problem, and Claymore encouraged her to find out what she could. They agreed to rendezvous on the Point of the Esplanade at noon.

Claymore waited in the open air, ocean behind her and a clear field of fire in front—for Sirich or anyone else who kept the appointment.

The woman known as "See" was in Special Projects when the urgent call from Intelligence reached her. Though she'd had many decades of experience controlling her emotions, she was angry. To participate in the experimental work in Special Projects was one of the few remaining pleasures in a life otherwise occupied by administrative trivia. She had left instructions that she was never to be disturbed during her rare, too-brief visits to the floor.

She took the call in the SP chief's office. Waiting for the connection, she lightly touched a finger to the little muscle between her brows, an old trick useful for releasing tension in the facial mask. This year her skin was smooth and brown, her hair long and black. She looked about thirty-five, an age appropriate to her presumed life history. Few people on Darwin knew her true age. Jim Asmussen of Intelligence was one of them, however.

The communicator block coagulated and Asmussen's features appeared. "I apologize, See, sincerely. But I have to know how you want to handle this."

"You wouldn't call if it weren't important," she said automatically.

"Yesterday Abramian picked up a couple of tourist applications with phony documentation. The counterfeit was superb. He says the computer wouldn't have caught it, except his people were tipped."

This was hardly news. As head of counter-smuggling operations Felix Abramian handled situations like this several times a month. See waited for the punch line.

"He sent a couple of plainclothes people over to the Burton this morning, but they only nabbed one of the suspects. She offered no resistance. In fact she claimed she was the one who tipped them. She asked to see Abramian in person. She asked for him by name, so naturally they complied."

"Where is she now?" See asked.

"In his office," said Asmussen. "When she got there she started giving him orders! She wants him to put the phony applications through. She wants him to 'stay out of her way for a couple of weeks'—her words. Though she did offer to check in with him once in awhile if he'd like."

"How considerate."

"She said if he had any questions he should ask me, and if *I* had any questions I should ask you."

"She knows who we are?"

"Here's her profile, See." Asmussen reached to the side; his image was replaced by a three-dimensional colored graph, a genetic abstract. Asmussen let it stay in view only a moment before he said, "And this is what she looks like in person—live from Felix's office."

The head of an old woman appeared in the communicator. She wore her salt and pepper hair cropped close, and she looked very old. She was smiling patiently.

"Okay, Jim, that's good enough," said See.

The old woman's image was replaced by Asmussen's face. He looked at his boss inquisitively.

She thought in silence. This wasn't in her plans; she had no explanation for it; she was mightily curious—it was the first really *new* situation she'd encountered in well over a century. She should pry into it, get all the details, all the whys and wherefores.

But she resisted the immediate prying urge. She was wise enough to know that wisdom came from patient observation. There was some deep game afoot, and clearly she would learn more if she did nothing more than wait. Meanwhile, why spoil the suspense?

"Give her what she wants, Jim," she said at last. She was surprised to find she felt like laughing. "I don't know what I'm up to or how I got here any more than you do, but I'm inclined to trust myself."

Asmussen nodded. "Right, Clarissa."

Claymore watched Sirich's erect, spry figure make brisk progress across the emerald lawns of the Esplanade. She'd kept the appointment to the minute. From the satisfied look on her face she'd accomplished whatever she'd set out to do. As she came up to Claymore she produced a pair of slim plastic code chips from her raincape pocket. "Unrestricted travel. *And* an apology for the delay."

"Excellent," said Claymore. It appeared Sirich had not betrayed her after all. "What was the problem with the documents?"

"Nothing. Your people had the right code, but we filed early, before the Customs computers were through processing. They bounced every application on the list—over six hundred people—and thought it was their own fault!"

Claymore sighed. Learning to hold steady and wait out the inevitable coincidences had been an early part of her training. So why this vague disappointment? Was she looking for trouble? Perhaps she'd hoped the mission wasn't going to be over with as quickly and efficiently as her superiors wanted.

From Sirich's eyes, bright with excitement, she realized the older woman was in no hurry to get back to Earth either. Claymore turned to stare at the gray cliffs across the water. The wind blew long strands of her auburn hair across her eyes; she reached up and hooked them out of the way. She wished she could stay here in Cuvier until the weather broke and the sun came out, until the rising sun shone full upon the glacier-crowned granite.

But she was not free to linger.

20

Holder stared at Phil in exasperation. "Not 120! You're supposed to be counting the permutations of five things, two of them equivalent to each other, and the other three also equivalent." Holder ran his tongue over his teeth; he could fight a crocodile for a double martini right now. It was hours until sundown, which would be strictly by the clock today, and no one on the expedition touched a drop before then.

Phil sat cross-legged on the plastic floor grid. His sullen expression was eloquent as he stared at the sheet of water pouring off the edge of the rolled-up tent wall only centimeters from his nose. Inside the tent the air was cool but sticky; outside, the dim outlines of other tents and the pale shapes of trees at the edge of the high meadow were barely visible through vertical curtains of rain.

They'd had to set up camp in the rain. They'd had to line up for most of their meals in the rain, waiting outside the mess tent huddled together in panchos that let water in at the neck, standing in mud up to their ankles.

"So?" Holder prodded, pressing the projector stud to make the aerial display wind back.

Phil refused to look at Holder, or allow the projector's beam to catch his eye. "So what?" he grumbled.

"So, five factorial has to be divided by two factorial times three factorial!" Holder sped through the simple equation, then yanked the mathfile out of the projector and tossed it angrily aside. It bounced off his tightly-made cot. "How many times do I have to repeat the same problem? How do you ever expect to be a biologist if you can't handle simple combinations?"

"The great *Darwin* didn't need math," Phil said sarcastically.

"Darwin needed it and he knew it," Holder snapped. "*He* at least was sufficiently intelligent to regret his ignorance."

The boy opened his mouth to say something, but then he turned away, humiliated.

Too late Holder repented; the slashing debater's style he'd honed in a lifetime of academic infighting was worse than useless to him here. He was making Phil hate math and every other subject he was trying to teach, just as Unwin had made him hate them.

Was the situation everything, then, and personality nothing? He would not believe it. He was simply not applying the lessons he should have learned from his own experience, even his experience of this very tent, this very rain.

He sighed heavily. "Let's drop the schoolwork for awhile, Phil," he said. "I don't like being cooped up like this any better than you do."

Still Phil said nothing. He sat as far away from Holder

as he could get, his chin planted on his hand, staring at the green wall of water and the gooey red mud it was churning into soup, and listening to the torrents of runoff that gurgled beneath the floorboards. Nothing could swim, fly, walk, or even comfortably sit still in weather like this. Except dinosaurs. They probably liked it. Off at the edge of camp the triceratops in the remuda looked positively frisky.

"So'd Frank take you to the site yesterday?" Holder asked, trying to sound casual.

"Yeah," Phil answered. He stirred at the mention of Frank's name, as Holder had hoped.

"It was nice of your Dad to give you a place in the cages," Holder continued cautiously, trying to draw Phil out.

"It's not exactly a *favor*. Dad knows I'm good with a recorder."

"He showed me some of your work. Excellent." Holder hoped he didn't sound insincere. He'd never thought that much of his own movies.

"Yeah, thanks." Phil rocked back on his hands. At the thought of the holography assignment his mood began to lighten. "It was probably Frank who gave Dad the idea. I know it was him that persuaded Mom to let me come. She doesn't want me to do anything."

"She has slightly different priorities, that's all."

"And Dad wouldn't even have stood up to her if it weren't for Frank," Phil went on, warming to his grievance. "Sometimes I wish . . ." He stopped.

(. . . that Frank was your father instead of Alex, thought Holder.) He changed the subject; to be party to Phil's disloyal thoughts was treading dangerous ground. "Why d'you think they picked that particular site?"

Phil looked at him directly at last. "You really don't know a whole lot about dinosaurs, do you?" He was honestly puzzled that a man of Unwin's inexperience should have gained such a high place in Alex Holder's estimation. Dumb luck was the only possible answer.

"I only know what I've learned since I've been on Darwin."

"Well . . . you know what *ethology* is?" Phil looked sidelong at Holder. Holder nodded. "Well, the site's perfect if you know a little bit of dinosaur ethology," said Phil, savoring the impressive word. "*Tyrannosaurus* isn't a social carnivore. Tyrannosaurs hunt alone usually, sometimes in pairs."

Phil warmed to the lecture with quick enthusiasm. Holder,

amused to recognize the roots of his own style, listened solemnly.

"They're good parents when the little ones are still little, but as soon as they get big enough to leave the nest the adults chase them off. And the ones that don't run fast enough get eaten. It takes a big range to support a rex, where the prey isn't artificially abundant—like around the hotels."

"That's not the case up here."

"No, this is really wild country. Even Rangers don't come up here much, except to do population counts. The dinosaurs are on their own, like Dad says. He's real proud of it. That means the rexes are going to have to work to survive."

"So Frank and your Dad picked especially good hunting grounds for the first transplants?"

Phil nodded. "A redwood valley, which means plenty of cover but not much undergrowth. And a resident herd of tops. The Rangers'll stake down some little tops until the rexes get used to eating them. After that they'll be on their own too." Phil paused, his glance flickering shyly away from Holder. "Mr. Unwin . . . T.T. . . ."

"Yes, Phil?"

"I'm sorry about before." He waved at the mathfile. "I know I've got to work at this stuff . . ." He ran out of words.

Holder felt a rush of gratitude. "It's the weather," he said. He wondered at Phil's sudden burst of maturity. For himself, he couldn't remember ever having the courage to face up to his own rudeness, but maybe Unwin had never given him an opening. "And I've got to admit I'm a lousy tutor. I'm more comfortable lecturing."

Adults rarely bothered even to explain themselves to Phil, much less apologize. He grinned, and held out his hand. "Shake?"

Holder looked at Phil, and for a moment there was no sound between them, only the drum and bubble of the steaming rain. Love welled up in him. He reached for Phil's hand . . .

. . . and as he touched it everything turned sour. Holder felt nauseous, unclean. He withdrew his trembling hand, felt his skin burn, sweat spring out on his forehead.

He staggered out of his chair with a stricken groan, avoiding the boy's shocked gaze. He brushed aside the netting at the entrance to the tent and lunged into the rain.

His feet sank deep into the mud; greasy rolls of it curled

over his boot tops. He staggered and fell to his hands and knees, losing one boot to the sucking mud. Water pounded his head and back. His ears roared. He retched.

Now Phil was beside him, laying a nervous hand on his shoulder. "Mr. Unwin? What's the matter? What . . .?"

Holder rolled away from him, shrinking from the awful touch of his Doppelgänger's hand.

He had committed an obscenity. He shriveled with revulsion; everything he was doing was an obscenity. He was vaguely aware of green and brown uniforms approaching through the exploding liquid veil of raindrops in front of his face. Could he recover before they found him out? He must force these thoughts, these disgusting thoughts, down and away before it was too late.

How dare he? How dare he love himself?

21

Once I had it right, and it was simple: all learning is the result of repetition, from the "learning" of the developing nervous system to the simple learning of stimulus and response, to the deep understanding of meta-learning. Wisdom results from encountering the same phenomena over and over again, turning them, as it were, in a crystal of differing contexts.

Holder and the medic knew there was nothing physically wrong with him; the medic called it "four-wall fever," gave him a note for some pills, and assured him he would feel better when the rain stopped. As if on cue, the rain did stop, and before sunset the sun peeked under the clouds.

Holder showed up at the quartermaster's tent as the expedition's big cargo helicopter was lifting off to take Frank Seaton back to Camp Owen Gorge, where he would fetch the first tyrannosaur. Li, the quartermaster, went to find Holder's packet of seasick pills. While Li was in the back of the tent looking for the seldom-used medicine, Holder prescribed for himself. He filched a liter of gin from the shelf under the counter and tucked it into his belt, under his voluminous rain slicker.

She showed me how I could make the ultimate test of my pat theories, how I could realize my obsession of returning, repeating, re-entering experience. Then I faced a choice: would I attempt to drastically alter the environment of my upbringing—kidnap myself, murder my father in the grand old Greek way? Or would I try to make a difference with small changes—like the random mutations that affect an individual's genetic and physical makeup, but are of no consequence to the species?

The bottle was half gone, and the pain had dulled, and the clouds were starting to break up and blow away. The moon, that intense, bright spark, played hide and seek as he sat huddled in the soggy eucalyptus. The wet leaves smelled sharply of urine, their natural odor—he had not lost complete control of himself, yet.

I didn't foresee this awful isolation. I had a vague faith in some kind of mystical identity of self with self. What nonsense! I'm two different people. I'm even allergic to myself! How's that for mystical identity?

Both of us are real, both of us have our own histories—only accidentally shared up to a point—both of us have our own concerns for the present and our own hopes for the future. Just because I know what his hopes are, just because they were mine once, doesn't alter our differences in the least. I can't tell my little twin brother of any of what I know, and he wouldn't believe me if I did . . .

The gin sloshed in the bottle, blue in the moonlight. Holder stared at it.

I wonder what he thinks of me? I hated Unwin at first. Maybe I never got over the resentment, though I started feeling sorry for him later.

Unwin's potential as a playmate was a lot greater than the little teacher robots I was used to, but that was offset—I craved my parents' acceptance, especially Dad's. I desperately wanted to impress them with my maturity, my personhood. Unwin got in the way of that, but good, with all his reports and helpful suggestions.

Oh, I hated the folks too, sometimes, for failing to be impressed. For insisting on treating me like a child. Oh, I'll do a lot better when I grow up, I said, My kid'll get the benefit of all their mistakes.

When it came to shaping Phil's future, though, he had only one advantage over Alex and Isabel. He knew the *events* of the future, and that was less of an advantage than one might suppose, since he couldn't tell anybody what he knew. Of course when he could remember clearly he knew exactly what Phil was thinking, but adolescents are notoriously easy to mind-read anyway. Countless generations of parents before him had learned to their sorrow that merely knowing what's on a kid's mind doesn't make him easier to talk to. It may make things worse.

Throughout months and years of planning Holder had had a thin, obligatory appreciation of the difficulties he would face. He'd been driven by the obsessive belief that somehow he would manage to overcome the barriers to communication. Instead, he found himself *in loco parentis.* "The Child is father of the man," the poet said. Now the man was father of himself.

Like a father, there were things he knew, experiences he'd had, agonies he'd endured, joys that had come upon him unexpectedly, all of which he wanted desperately to convey to this still unformed, not quite innocent being who was *him.*

He took another sip.

Tell the truth, I even hate him. I hate him for all the things he hasn't done yet but will do because I can't figure out how to stop him. Stop myself.

Himself, myself, the other Unwin, the No Win, the No One. I'm a supernumerary in this universe, I've violated the Conservation Laws. Not the laws of mass/energy conservation, to be sure—with all the stuff that's constantly falling into and out of black holes, one extra human body a little out of its time and place is an insignificant, temporary statistical anomaly. The Conservation Laws I've violated are of a higher order; they are the laws of Psychic Conservation: there shall be a constant ratio of Beings to Persons, one to one, per Universe. Extra souls are forbidden, and where they occur shall undergo spontaneous decay.

And yet another sip. Rather more than a sip.

The night was only half gone. He'd better make this bottle last. Might last if he got started walking now. The moon was bright, the clouds were all blown to tatters. He knew the path down to the redwood valley; he remembered it very well.

Small changes all very well, but not enough, not fast enough—got to make this damned world work right, and fast.

Holder jammed the bottle inside his coat, cuddling it close to his tummy, keeping it nice and warm. He struggled to his feet, pointed himself in the right direction, and lurched off resolutely into the night forest.

22

Above Seaton's head the twin rotors of the big cargo helicopter rhythmically shredded the morning sunshine, spilling shards of light over his shoulders and arms. His instruments, plus his practiced ear, reassured him that the copter's supercooled magnets and miniaturized fusion-pak were feeding the blade-tip steam jets with flawless efficiency. Through the clear plastic blister he watched the landscape unfold ahead: it was an abrupt landscape, criss-crossed with lava flows and ravines and dotted with cinder cones, all thickly covered with trackless heterogeneous forest.

Suspended beneath the helicopter in a cradle of polysteel mesh, swaying gently in the breeze, lay 9,000 kilograms of sleeping *Tyrannosaurus*. The tranquilizing cocktail administered to the animal back at Camp Owen Gorge was due to start wearing off in fifteen minutes. Seaton planned to be on the ground in five minutes, and off again in ten.

The communicator chimed. "We hear you down canyon, Frank," Alex's voice announced. "Right on schedule."

"I'm starting my descent," Seaton said. He guided the chopper lower into the wide canyon. Half a millennium earlier a great lava flow had stopped here, its leading edge forming long fingers of high black volcanic rock. Between two of these mesas was the chosen canyon, thick with oak and laurel and redwood. The tallest trees dated from the earliest years of the terraforming of Bounty, and grew to heights of over a hundred meters.

"Frank, you should be aware that we're missing Unwin," said Alex. "I assigned him to the base camp for the duration, but I just got a report he's turned up absent."

"Okay, Alex." Now Seaton could see the clearing, a patch of wet grass steaming with mist in the morning light, ringed with bristling cycads and bright pink clumps of rhododendron. Down through the trees he caught sight of one of the observation cages, the one that Alex and young Phil were using, stationed in the path the tyrannosaur was expected to take once it woke up. Farther down the canyon, along the same path, the Rangers had staked out a baby tops; the hapless creature would provide breakfast for the half-starved carnosaur.

This early the ground mist was still thick, and Seaton hoped it wouldn't interfere with young Phil's holography; it meant a lot to the boy to do a good job. The ground had been thoroughly soaked by the thunderstorms of the last several days. Though the rain had caused the theropod expedition considerable inconvenience, Seaton knew no one could do anything about the weather—the Central Environmental Council wouldn't allow it. Oh, they occasionally permitted fine tuning of climate on a continental scale, but day to day tinkering with the weather was a farmer's vice, a sure path to perdition.

The helicopter was clear of the trees now, flying below the tops of the tallest of them. Downdrafts from the rotors caused the mist to curl up in great curving festoons. Seaton circled the clearing slowly, his full concentration on the dangerous task of landing the heavy machine. With no fossil fuels at all on Darwin, and with clean fusion-paks notoriously cranky to maintain, a helicopter was a rare and valuable piece of machinery—only two were assigned to Cretacia. Below a hundred meters, with no forward airspeed, a power failure could be disastrous: there would be no time to jettison the load and let autorotation retard the fall.

But it was Seaton's job to deposit his big baby with all due delicacy, so he came in slowly.

Kani alone of all the people knew that even at this moment a tyrannosaur was among them. He had seen it descending from the sky in lazy splendor, and judging by the sound of the sky machine when it went out of sight the creature must be nearing the ground even now, and not too far away.

There were Rangers all around him, though—the place stank of them—so he must proceed with extreme care.

Again the wicked thought tempted him: things were happening so fast, much faster than the Trader said they would, and he was the only one to know, and the blood of *Tyrannosaurus* was powerful magic. If somehow he were to slay it before any of the others knew of its existence, and make a personal thanks . . .

But the people would not thank *him* if he frightened off the Rangers before they brought more tyrannosaurs, or if he frustrated the Traders' desires for hides. Mother Ariana herself had given him his instructions: he was to learn the details of the Rangers' plans, and plot the whereabouts of the new animals. He was not to interfere in any way.

He really knew nothing about tyrannosaurs anyway, or how they behaved, except what the old legends told. He badly needed to find out more. He moved stealthily toward the distant sound of the sky machine's engines.

In the shadow of the deep woods the sound of the circling machine was muffled. Fascinated, Holder watched the naked blond boy move among the misty redwoods. The performance amazed him, partly because Holder was drunk, but partly because it was a truly amazing performance.

Except for an occasional cycad, the eternal shade of the big trees prohibited all but a thin ground cover of ferns and moss—nothing much to hide behind. The boy depended only on silence, and a seemingly instinctive ability to pose himself against the backdrop of tall ruddy columns and threads of mist and shafts of pallid sunlight in such a way as to blend into the pattern of light and dark. If one did not suspect his presence—and he had every right to assume that no one did—he was as well hidden as the mosaic numbers in a color-blind test are to the color-blind.

Holder utterly lacked the boy's skill at woodcraft, even when stone sober, but he had the advantage of knowing where to wait before the boy had thought of going there. As quietly as he could, Holder now moved to interpose himself between the young "barbarian" and the deadly creature he stalked.

He intended to save that fool's neck. Nothing would change in the reality Holder had grown up in, but as his mentor had continually drummed into him, Reality is the reality where you are.

He wasn't doing it for the boy's sake, not altogether. His own worldline had been a moving nexus of death, starting on that long-ago analogue of this very day. Death was a function of his presence; he intended to reverse the sign of the deadly function for the Phil Holder of this Reality—therefore he was still acting on behalf of himself, however that slippery concept was defined.

Under the chopper's belly the solenoids snapped the safety bolts back and the shackles parted, allowing the metal net to collapse over the body of the dinosaur. Instantly the fluttering shriek of the rotors changed pitch and the chopper slid up and away, over the tree tops toward bare ground at the rim of the nearest mesa. Seaton would park the craft overlooking the canyon until it was clear he was no longer needed.

Rangers rushed through the ground fog to tug at the heavy netting that covered the animal, pulling it away and spreading it flat on the ground. With quick hammer blows of trenching tools they began pegging the edges of the net to the ground, to keep the animal from tangling itself when it woke. They had only a few minutes. The operation had been timed to minimize the period the tyrannosaur would lie torpid on the ground, its heart and lungs straining against its own crushing weight.

The last metal peg went home as the massive legs and tail quivered and the ghastly jaws opened convulsively. The men and women scattered and ran for the protective cages.

The Rangers had offered a baby triceratops to the tyrannosaur, Kani noted with approval, even though its pitiful squeals made him uneasy. He circled the chained animal at a distance.

Now he needed only to find an appropriate hiding place. Surely at any moment the tyrannosaur would come this way, attracted by the staked prey. Kani took a soundless step forward. The brush crackled in front of him. He froze.

Bright green fernlike fronds of redwood shoots, sprouting from a nurse log, suddenly parted. A horrid old demon rose up pointing a weapon at him. "If you know what this is, boy, you'll run for your life."

Phil shuddered with excitement as redwood branches whipped aside and he found himself staring down the pink throat of the tyrannosaur. He glanced at the instruments on the recording gear that, along with himself, his father, and two other Rangers, filled the observation cage to capacity. The recorder was getting it all, a perfect pickup.

The giant bellowed and exploded from the trees, taking three frighteningly rapid strides forward. The ground shook each time a clawed foot hit the ground. The nightmare animal stopped briefly in the middle of the mossy little clearing, its red expressionless eyes staring fixedly from under bony orbital ridges. Its mouth hung open, and its breath came in liquid grunts.

"What a shot!" Phil exclaimed, forgetting himself.

"Silence!" Alex hissed angrily.

"Alex," said Seaton's voice on the communicator.

"You could have picked a better time, Frank," Alex whispered. "What the hell is it?" He didn't look at Frank's image in the communicator block, but kept his eyes trained upward through the bars at the dinosaur that towered over them.

"I can see Unwin from up here," Seaton said. "And somebody with him. They just went past the little tops, running. If the rex don't stop . . ."

"Thanks, Frank, we'll follow it up."

The tyrannosaur roared, and from the depths of the woods came the terrified bleat of the captive triceratops calf. The tyrannosaur charged past the cage into the shadows of the forest.

Alex threw back the bolt on the cage door and shoved a rocket launcher into the woman Ranger's hands. "Take the south wall, Shanta." He grabbed a dart gun from the rack and thrust it at the man. "Em, you take the north. Don't wait for me, I'll slow you down." He grabbed Shanta's wrist as she started through the door and pointed at the launcher. "Safety off. Shoot to save Unwin's life, if you have to. I'll take it out of his hide later." He left the cage behind them, turning to slam the door shut just as Phil started to follow. "Stay in here, Phil. Hear me?"

Phil stepped back into the cage, speechless with shame and fury. He watched his father stump off down the path the carnosaur and the pursuing Rangers had taken. Hell, he could take better care of himself than that half-crippled old man. Damn him! And damn Unwin!

Unwin had done it again. He'd stolen the spotlight with his insane antics. . . .

Kani ran as fast as he could, making no effort to hide or be silent. Branches whipped his face and bare chest as he ran.

A dead bough scraped across him and yanked the rope from his shoulder—he flung it aside lest it tangle him.

The shadowed woods behind him were howling with silent monsters. He could feel the breath of hot-blooded dinosaurs on his shoulders. He anticipated the searing agony of a fire bolt from the demon's weapon at any moment, for now he credited everything he'd ever heard of the demon Rangers. He did not look back. He simply ran.

After many minutes of running he began to think perhaps he had managed to outdistance his pursuers. He wondered if he dared slow down long enough to look; despite his frank terror he was mightily curious.

He must have deeply offended the Goddess by merely toying with the notion of disobedience, by just thinking of killing the tyrannosaur—as if he could possibly have done so! Nevertheless, he did not question that he deserved death.

But possibly it was not her purpose to kill him; perhaps the demon had been sent only to warn him away.

Ahead, where the valley widened and the north wall was always in sunlight, the redwoods thinned and gave way to a grove of oaks. Kani left the shadow of the evergreens and ran in among the twisting trunks. If anything had pursued him this far he would have heard it now, crashing through the dead leaves thick on the ground or shattering the brittle branches above. Yet he heard only his own footsteps, and his sobbing breath. He slowed; he faltered to a standstill. He turned, fearfully, and looked behind him.

He saw nothing. But he heard a drumming as of great wings, a thin unceasing scream. The sky machine . . .

With mounting terror he felt the truth uncoil in him. They were coming from the air. Even as he took a tentative step back toward the darkness of the big trees, hoping to find sanctuary in the shadows, the old demon staggered out of the ruddy gloom a dozen paces away. Red-faced and gasping, the old one hardly looked formidable now. "Run, fool!" he screeched. "Don't you know what will happen to you? What will happen to all of you? Run!"

Kani could barely decipher the harsh garbled words, but he turned. The aircraft was louder, and coming closer. A woman black as all the Rangers emerged from the forest a hundred paces to the south. She called something, something strident he could not understand, and waved the long tube weapon in her hand.

And now to the north another Ranger appeared, pointing a weapon and shouting into the roar of the machine.

And overhead, through the limbs of the trees, the sky darkened with the shadow of the flying machine, and a black face grimaced at him from the machine's single eye, and the air was filled with the clatter and scream of vast flickering wings. A great hot wind arose, blinding him with dust and summoning uncounted dead oak leaves to dance a devil's mocking dance around him.

"O divine Goddess Mother Bounty take my soul," Kani cried, and fell trembling to earth.

23

"Got a little problem here. Calls for strategy."

The computer said nothing. Langoza hadn't asked it a question yet. He drummed his fingers on the arm of the pilot's seat, his swarthy face illuminated by the green glow from the airplane's control console. Through the plane's windows he could see the village hearthfires glowing deep within the shadows of the rocky cleft, visible from the plane's parking place but hidden, even at night, from the forest and sky above.

Langoza leaned back and rested his chin on the tips of his fingers. "Okay. This kid the Mother sent out to spy on the Rangers got himself caught. Them two warriors she sent to keep an eye on him, Meria, and Leri I think the guy's name is, they brought her the news. They were real hot to go after the kid, set him loose. She says no, whatever happens is destined or something. To me she says, very sorry, looks like no rex hides for you, see you next year and thanks so much for the beads." Langoza snorted. "No rex hides! Do you *know* what I can get for a rex hide on Epsilon Eridani these days?"

"Yes," the computer said in its bland, machine-standard voice. "According to data current at the time of our last departure, on the Eridanian black market the uncured hide of a large *Tyrannosaurus rex* is worth approximately 10,000 Eridanian cents. A cured hide..."

"My point exactly." Langoza nodded. Then his features twisted, indignant. "So who does this Mother think she is, telling me to take off?"

"Traditionally, the Mother Ariana regards herself, and is regarded by her followers, as..."

"Rhetorical," Langoza snapped. Idiot machine.

He got out of his chair, paced the few short steps to the back of the cabin, then returned to the couch. "Okay. I've seen this coming for years. This Mother's got some kind of fancy idea of doing away with us middlemen. That's one good reason to get rid of her, right there. And her people are sitting right on the territory I'm interested in most. That's an even better one. The question is, what's the best way to do it?"

"In taking any action the first consideration must be to avoid bringing suspicion on ourselves," said the computer.

"Brilliant," Langoza muttered.

"Therefore it would be advantageous to incite the Rangers to kill or capture all of the Mother Ariana's people, but to do so for motives unrelated to Trader activities."

"Terrific. Keep thinking."

"We have on board four cases of government issue rocket launchers, removed from stores at Copeville."

Langoza's black eyebrows rose. What was his damned machine cooking up? "State of the art, those are. Should be worth a pile to the rebels on Brindle. Didn't I sure as hell pay that Ranger enough for 'em?"

"Yes, You paid him 40,000 Darwinian cents. Recent rebel bids have been in the 200,000 cent range. Adjusting for overhead and expenses and current rates of exchange..."

"Get to the point."

"Give one rocket launcher and a supply of unfused rockets to the warriors Leri and Mera. Using the following arguments, induce them to attack the Ranger camp on their own initiative..."

"Hang on a second. Do that and the Rangers'll wipe out the Mother's people, okay, but they'll trace that gun right back to that Ranger, Sammy. Hell, they'll think *he* sold 'em the gun!"

The computer had not been programmed to reply to truisms.

After a moment Langoza got the point. "Okay. I guess it won't be too hard to shut Sammy up before he spills. Tell me what I'm supposed to say to them fucking savages. . . ."

Holder was conscious of the stark moonlight, the black shapes of the trees, the distant snort and shuffle of penned triceratops, the few stars bright enough to shine in the moon-softened night. He was also conscious of his own stink, and his soiled, crumpled clothes, and the throbbing headache that marked the return of sobriety.

Beside him he felt the looming taciturn presence of Mamaka, Alex's top wrangler. A few meters away the entrance of the administration tent spilled blue light on the moist earth. The fabric of the tent glowed a softer blue.

Holder registered all these things, but they suggested nothing to him. He had been cut adrift in a universe of unpredictable phenomena.

Voices drifted to him from the tent, low, indistinct, soured with anger. Soon he would be thrust into that vat of emotion, for the third time that day. Meanwhile he waited, without hope or plan for the future.

The Chief Ranger grasped the necklace of teeth in his thick dark fist and jerked. The boy's head snapped forward, but the necklace did not break.

Shanta looked up from the monitoring instruments on the camp table in front of her. "Chief," she said, alarmed. "The record . . ."

Furious, Alex yanked again, harder. The leather thong parted. Teeth flew across the tent, bouncing from the drum-tight walls, clattering on the plastic flooring. Bright swelts stood out on the back of the boy's neck.

In his clenched fist Alex still held three of the curved teeth, each several centimeters long. The necklace's broken thong hung limp. "Where did you get these, you little bare-ass bastard?" His low voice was choked with temper. "Did you kill for them? Did you kill an animal so you could hang these around your pale primitive neck?"

The boy said nothing. He had said nothing during the last session either, or the one before that. His eyes were downcast, his blond mustaches drooped, the muscles of his arms quivered with tension and fatigue; he had not responded even when the Rangers had offered him food.

Shanta tried again. "Chief, I respectfully suggest . . ."

Alex swung around and shook the fistful of teeth at her. "These are a gorgo's teeth. Five months to grow a gorgo in the vats, and this son-of-a-bitch kills one to make himself pretty." He glared at her. Her eyes dropped.

He shifted his gaze to Emerson, his laboratory chief. "Well, Em? You've got an investment in this." But Emerson would not meet his eyes.

"He didn't kill no gorgo, Alex," said Seaton, matter-of-factly. Seaton was stretched out in a camp chair by the entrance, his thumbs hooked in his trouser pockets. "There's no gorgos around here. And that boy's not dressed for traveling."

"Then he killed something else to trade for them," Alex said angrily. "A few tops, maybe. Ankylosaurs. Scolosaurs. Even a big croc. Scum smugglers buy them all. *He kills animals,* Frank."

"Okay, Alex," said his friend, soothing him with his voice. "But the poor dumb son-of-a-bitch doesn't know any better, you can tell just by looking at him." He grinned ruefully to emphasize his point. "Now you know Cuvier's waiting on us, Alex. When can I tell Re-ed we'll hand him over?"

"When he tells us where the rest of them are," the Chief Ranger said. "Frank, I won't have that nice-folks-like-us shit you're peddling."

"Don't shush me, Alex Holder, when I'm standing between you and a criminal charge." Seaton sat up in his chair. "This boy won't eat. He's dead on his feet, but he won't close his eyes. I think he's beggin' somebody to kill him, Alex, and it better not be one of us."

Alex jerked away from Seaton's blunt plain face. He didn't want to hear reason. He pushed his own face close to the exhausted prisoner's. "You're lower than any animal," he whispered. The spittle balled at the corners of his mouth. "I'll find all of you people and clean you out of my country for good." He stepped away, still glaring at the barbarian. "Take him, Frank," he said at last. "Lock him up in the chopper."

Seaton stood. "Cuvier, Alex?"

"Tomorrow." Alex sounded defeated. "Call Re-ed, have them meet you at the Camp."

Seaton looked at the prisoner, "Come here, kid." But the boy still looked at the floor. Seaton stepped forward and gently took him by the upper arm. Passively, the boy followed Seaton toward the entrance.

"Unwin again," Alex said.

Seaton pulled the tent flaps back to reveal Holder already standing there, his face pale with doom—Mamaka had anticipated his Chief's command. Seaton led the naked boy past Holder, into the night.

Holder entered, nudged by Mamaka. He squinted at the bright lights. Alex reached out to Shanta's console and hit a switch with the flat of his palm.

"You can't do that, Chief," Shanta said nervously. "The time code will show the lapse."

"The batteries exploded," Alex said calmly. "You were burned and had to seek medical attention. Emerson, you too."

Shanta and Emerson exchanged glances. Emerson's face twitched with indecision; unlike Seaton, he had no experience talking back to his administrative superiors. He half shrugged.

Shanta looked away from him, disgusted by his cowardice, though no less frightened of Alex. "What about him?" she asked Alex, looking at Holder. "Did he get hurt too?"

Alex stared at Holder. "I don't know yet. I think we just had a quiet chat while you two were off getting bandages on your scrapes. When you came back the equipment was working again and Mr. Whoever-he-is was making a full statement."

Shanta drew a breath, summoning her courage. "If that's not what happens, Chief, *I'm* prepared to make a statement. A full and truthful statement. Even if it means my job. Even if it means yours."

"Thank you, Shanta," said Alex. "Go get that bump attended to."

"I'll be right outside," she said.

"Just get out."

She and the sheepish Emerson went quietly.

Alex jerked his chin at Mamaka and the guard shifted his grip on Holder; a massive fist curled around each of Holder's elbows.

Alex stepped closer and lowered his voice. "Better be sober enough to talk, mister. I want to find out what you're doing in my family. I want to find out what you're doing with my boy. The rest I'll leave to Re-ed. But they'll never see you if you don't talk to me."

Holder's fear crystalized—not because of Alex's threats, though he had no doubt of the man's sincerity; plainly Alex had crossed that line where rage feeds on self-justification. But the magnitude of what, in his drunkenness, he had taken on himself stood suddenly revealed. What happened to the feral boy and his people was now totally his responsibility. And *Phil*—in addition to everything else, Phil would find himself embroiled in an inexplicable violation of the Uniform Code, if Holder allowed anyone on Darwin to take his own genetic profile, alive or dead.

Alex slapped him hard. "Come on, mister, you're running short of time."

Holder's cheek stung and his eyes watered. On top of everything else, he had to keep Alex out of trouble. For Phil's sake he had to come up with something that would placate Alex, save face, and incidentally give himself time to plan an escape.

". . . what's the matter, are they unhappy with the way I'm doing things? The new Commissioners are a lot farther toward the edge than the old ones, aren't they, Mamaka? But this character's too weak and disorganized to be anything like that, too dumb, too soft to be a spy. . ."

"Not the kind you think," said Holder.

". . . so who the hell are you?" Alex finished, before he heard the answer. "What did you say?"

Why had he said that? What could he make of it? Not the truth, surely! "They don't train professors in subversive techniques," Holder mumbled from a sore mouth. "And not in self-discipline, either."

"You're a professor?"

No, after all, the truth was simply impossible. "I'm an anthropologist."

"An *anthropologist!?*" Alex's composure wobbled. "They went out with organized religion!"

Holder attempted a grin. "No, that's missionaries." The grin hardened. "Primitives get them confused."

Alex didn't move.

Holder knew his father well; he pressed the advantage. "Is it only non-resistance that brings out the carnivore in you, Alex?" The more he tried to make Alex lose his temper, the calmer Alex would behave, to spite him. Holder felt perversely powerful; how very simple it was to play on his father's anger! But it was not a game to be played by anyone with anything to lose.

"Who are you? Where are you from?" Alex's dark face was darker with blood. "Are you some kind of queer like that guy you pretended to be?"

"My name is Evan Bruneau," Holder said quickly, and so calmly he surprised himself. "I'm an associate professor of anthropology at the University of Epsilon Eridani. I have no intrinsic interest in your family, Ranger Holder."

"Keep talking, mister."

Holder twisted in Mamaka's grasp. "I'm tired, Alex. Can I sit down?"

Alex nodded; his glittering black eyes were iron studs in a wooden mask.

Mamaka stepped back and Holder sagged onto a camp chair. His head lolling, he rubbed his neck with both hands. He began to speak. "I came to study the feral people, the ones you call barbarians. . ."

"I call them squatters."

". . . like that boy you captured. But I couldn't do it legally. The government of Darwin doesn't admit they exist." He tried to play it close to the truth, in case he had to repeat himself. "I bribed Unwin to let me take his place—I knew him slightly from the University, and I thought if I could get his job with his credentials it might put me in a good position to contact the feral people. They aren't all that much different from you, you know. I bet that boy's great-great-grandparents were runaways from the soleri that stood where you live now. They have a right . . ."

"They have no *right* to live anywhere," said Alex.

"You're conservators, all of you, unwilling to let go of the past," Holder said bitterly. "You seek a mythic perfection, attempting to recreate something that's dead and gone." Momentarily he was giddy with irony. He was repeating words that had been used to challenge his motives, to test his will when he'd first sought help on his mad quest. "Don't you find something faintly ridiculous, Alex, in the notion of a *tame* dinosaur?"

"Just talk."

More half-truths. "I was hoping I could befriend that lad I found wandering in the woods, keep him out of your sight. I thought he might eventually lead me to his tribe."

"Unhappily, you were drunk," Alex sneered. Clearly he knew the nature of the temptation; perhaps he was overproud of his own ability to resist.

"Yes, I botched it. But then that's the story of my life."

"We were simply a vehicle for you, Professor? My son and I?"

"You were the vector. I was the disease."

"How well you put it." Alex reached out and flipped on the recording gear. "This machine has been out of operation, on my orders," he announced for the holographic record. "Call back Shanta and Em, Mamaka."

Mamaka left the tent.

"To recapitulate our conversation of the last couple of minutes," Alex said calmly, "you claim to be an anthropologist from the University of Epsilon Eridani, by the name of . . . again, please?"

"Bruneau. Evan Bruneau. B-R-U-N-E-A-U." Holder was pleased; Alex seemed convinced.

"Here to study illegal squatters, 'feral people' as you call them. For this purpose, Professor Bruneau, you have seen fit to violate Darwinian law and the administrative regulations of this district—gravely, and on numerous occasions."

Shanta peered into the tent. She entered quickly, sat at her console, and made a few proprietary adjustments to the controls. Mamaka came in after her and stood silently by the entrance.

Alex looked at Shanta. "Where's Em?"

"At the infirmary. He's literal-minded. His burns, scrapes, and bumps will be a part of his permanent medical record."

Alex shook his head. He turned back to Holder. "Professor, you can make a statement for the record if you'd like. If you've been mistreated, threatened, that kind of thing . . .?"

Holder shook his head. What a simple man, for a man so complicated!

"You want to add anything to my summary?"

"I have a hunch I'll be repeating myself a lot, later on."

"Oh, indeed," Alex said, with some malice. "If Epseridan confirms your story, the diplomats will have a field day. Maybe Epseridan will decide you're not worth the risk, Professor. Maybe they'll claim they never heard of you."

Holder sighed. "You may be right."

Alex's dark smile expressed grim anticipation. "Want to change your story again, Mr. Un . . . Professor *Bruneau?*"

For a moment Holder actually considered it, considered trying the whole truth—that would certainly throw the Darwinian bureaucracy off the track for a few days! If anything could.

But he could do himself no good, and do none for young Phil, by playing the madman.

"No further statement, Ranger Holder."

24

"What's going to happen to him, Dad?" Phil sat on his bunk, looking past his father at the empty bunk across the tent.

Alex seemed too edgy to sit down, though pouches of fatigue showed beneath his eyes. "We'll turn him over to Re-ed tomorrow. Don't worry about him. I didn't come by to talk about him, really, I just wanted to make sure you were . . . that there was nothing you needed to tell me."

"About what, Dad?"

"Well, that man. He's acted pretty strangely the last couple of days, made a public spectacle of himself. He didn't . . ." Alex struggled with the distasteful subject. "He didn't act, uh, out of line with you, did he, son?"

"Well, no, I don't think so." Phil wasn't sure what his father was driving at. "He always seemed unhappy about something. I mean, sometimes he made me feel I was letting him down some way. But I think he liked me."

"How do you mean?" Alex asked. "Did he do anything?"

"No, really. He was just—he was honest."

"Honest!"

"I mean, he told me what was on his mind, and he always knew what was on mine. He was pretty funny sometimes, kidding me. And he was always *pushing* me, like he had faith I could do things that I wasn't sure I could. Stuff like that. I just felt he liked me." Phil wasn't sure his father was really hearing what he was trying to tell him.

"That's fine, then," Alex said, distracted. "I'll let you get some sleep, Phil." He stepped back, pushing the tent flap aside.

"Wait a second, Dad," said Phil. "What about that other guy. The savage?"

"What about him?" said Alex impatiently.

"I've heard people talking."

"Yes?"

Phil had been lying in the dark, and men and women too excited to sleep had passed outside his tent, half whispering, unaware anyone was awake to hear them. He had heard fear, and something else: an elliptical anticipation—of a hunt, of a slaughter. The music of their words was evil.

When a Ranger wanted to express violent contempt, "savage" was second only to "scum smuggler." Phil had never had to face the fact that savages were real people. He didn't like to think what his father might do to real people who acted the way savages were said to behave—killing precious animals.

"Nothing, Dad. I'll see you in the morning."

Alex paused a moment. Something was bothering Phil, that was obvious. But it didn't seem pressing, and other matters were. "All right, Phil. Good night." Alex let the tent flap fall closed behind him.

Phil lay back on his bunk, turning his face to the wall. Pale blobs of blue, refracted into four-pointed starbursts by the woven fabric of the tent, marked the location in the night of other tents whose inhabitants would not sleep. The administration tent was already dark, however. Tonight it was serving as a jail.

Why had Unwin—whoever he really was—why had he concerned himself with savages? How had he known the savage boy was out there in the valley? He must have known it in advance; he could never have stumbled on a savage by accident.

Who was Unwin? Unwin, who knew the ways of savages, though he claimed to know nothing of this planet, this continent, even of dinosaurs.

Dad said he'd taken all that back, that now he claimed to be some kind of scientist. But that sounded like just another tall tale.

Phil kicked at his cover and sat up again. When the chances of seeing Unwin again had suddenly grow remote, something had become clear: in spite of everything, the man was his friend. He had questions for his friend, and very little time left to get answers.

His heart was pounding as he crawled the last damp meter on muddy knees and elbows. He reached out and touched the back wall of the admin tent. His nails skritched on the fabric. "Mr. Unwin? T.T.?"

"Phil?" The hoarse whisper from the other side of the thin wall was barely audible. "What are you doing here?"

"I wanted to talk to you before they took you away." Phil put his mouth close to the wall. "Did they inject you with a tracer, T.T.?"

"No, Phil." Unwin's whisper sounded almost amused. "I don't think they were planning on taking prisoners when we came up here."

"Since they didn't . . ." Phil paused tentatively. "Would you like to get out of there?"

"Yes," came the answer, quick and intense.

"Move away from the wall. I'll slit the . . ."

"No!" Unwin's voice rose above a whisper, then dropped back. "There's a charge on the mesh. Don't perturb the field —I set it off once already tonight."

"Can you tell if Mamaka's awake?"

"He's asleep, I think. But I'm taped to the tent rib. If I pull away I'll break it."

"I'll kill the power and cut you loose."

"Can you get past him?"

"Sure. It's hard to wake him up when he's really asleep. Wait."

Phil crawled along the side of the tent until he reached the front. Cautiously he poked his head around the corner.

In front of him was the open field in the center of the encampment, a once-grassy meadow plowed into muddy chaos by the feet of humans and dinosaurs. Tents ringed the field, most of them dark. At each end of the field a hooded lamp stood on a tall standard, burning with a directionless white glare; the big cargo helicopter was parked under the nearer lamp, its long blades drooping, its polished aluminum skin reflecting the lights.

Though shadows moved in some of the tents, no one was on the field. Phil wriggled around the corner to the entrance of the administration tent, and paused long enough to listen to Mamaka's even, natural breathing. Cautiously he lifted the flap, revealing Mamaka's muddy boot, heel on the floor, toe in the air.

Phil pulled himself into the tent, sidling around the boots, inching forward until he estimated he was in the middle of the floor. He raised himself to his hands and knees and crawled slowly toward the back of the tent, feeling his way around chairs and table legs, gingerly lifting his bare knees over dusty electrical cables taped in bunches to the floor.

Under one table he found the wire he was looking for, felt along it up to a tiny generator set on the edge of the table, fumbled for the tab on the face of the device until he was sure he had the right switch, and killed the alarm.

By now his eyes were accustomed to the darkness. He could make out Unwin sitting with his knees drawn up, his ankles taped together, and his hands pulled behind him tightly where he was fastened to the tent upright. He was bound as securely as any dangerous prisoner.

Silently Phil felt for the tape on Unwin's ankles, then quickly sliced it away with his pocket knife. He moved closer, feeling behind Unwin for the knot of tape at his wrists. He could smell a rancid, fruity odor of sweat and old liquor, and he could hear Unwin's wheezing breath. He held his own breath while he cautiously sawed at the sticky tape.

Finally it was cut through. For a moment Unwin didn't move; then, painfully, he rolled forward onto his hands and knees, and crept after Phil.

They didn't stand fully upright until they reached the shelter of the eucalyptuses. Still they had to move cautiously—the way was choked with myriad slender eucalyptus shoots standing straight up, forming a labyrinth of vertical bars. Leathery sickle-shaped leaves and acorn-sized nuts covered the soggy ground. Finally they found a small dark clearing deep in the woods, and sat.

Unwin shuddered. "Thanks, Phil." He paused. "You wanted to talk? I guess I owe you."

"Who are you?"

"You do come to the point." His voice was choked. "I'm not really anybody, Phil. I can't tell you any more than that."

Phil knew he would never get the answers to all his questions. Perhaps Unwin couldn't answer them; but he wanted something for his efforts. "What's going to happen to the savages? Do you know?"

"Not really. But Alex wouldn't deliberately kill anyone."

"Do you believe what they're saying? That if the savages fight back . . ."

"I don't want to." Unwin rubbed his wrists mechanically.

"You always told me the truth, T.T."

"Leave it, Phil. I can't read the future. Not any more."

They were silent. The stars glistened cold and remote; the eucalyptus smell was bitter in the chill air.

Unwin broke the silence. "And there are no savages, Phil. Only savage acts."

"I didn't mean . . ."

"I know you didn't. But I want you to remember that, if you forget everything else."

"You came here to save those, uh, feral people. Didn't you?"

Unwin was quiet a very long time. When he finally spoke it had nothing to do with the question he'd been asked. "I've enjoyed the time we've had, Philip Holder. With luck you'll grow up to be a good man. God, I wish . . ."

"What, T.T.?"

"Nothing. You'll be a good man, Phil, I know it."

Unwin's expression of that thought made Phil queasy. Abruptly he got to his feet. He startled something small and mammalian in the darkness; he heard a furtive rattle and scurry in the leaves.

"Time you got some sleep," Unwin said for him. "Thanks for the furlough."

"Sure. Goodbye, T.T." Phil looked at him huddled in the darkness. What would become of him? He turned nervously and walked away. He took only a few steps before he stopped and turned again. "T.T.?"

"Yeah, Phil?"

"Good luck. Thanks."

"Do me a favor, Phil. Try to forget I ever existed."

Phil was torn between staying to comfort the mysteriously desolate man and the knowledge that he had nothing to offer him. He walked away.

Barely had Phil's head touched his pillow when the night erupted.

The roof of his tent lit with diffuse orange light, and he heard shouting—first one man, then two, then a woman's harsh challenge. Then the triceratops started bellowing, drowning everyone else.

He poked his head out of the tent flap, but he could see nothing clearly, only intermittent flares of red light illuminating the trees beyond the field. A bolt from a firegun blossomed beside the mounted floodlight near the helicopter, but did no damage.

The shouts and flares suddenly quieted, and only the belligerent trumpeting of the animals continued.

Phil turned and fished around on the floor of the tent for the shorts he had so recently shucked off. He pulled them back on and thrust his bare feet into his boots, then stumbled out of the tent.

Frank Seaton was striding toward him. Phil stopped in his tracks. What was Frank doing here? Catching sight of him, Frank beckoned with a jerk of his thumb. "Let's go, Phil. Your Dad wants a word with you."

25

The helicopter bounded smoothly from the dewy ground, beating upward through a broken layer of fluffy cumulus into a clear eastern sky. Soon the Ranger encampment was far below. The silver machine was alone above the clouds with the great purple cone of Owen; beyond the mountain the rising heraldic sun hurled rays of golden light through the tenuous clouds of morning.

Seaton piloted the copter in silent concentration, helmeted and visored against the dazzling light. Beside him in the right seat Phil sat brooding, stunned by the series of events that had put him here.

He had been prepared to take full responsibility for freeing Unwin, even knowing that the odds against a lone man in the wilderness were poor. He hadn't been prepared for Unwin to steal Mamaka's gun and free the savage. So many bolts were fired last night, so many tents went up in flames, it was a miracle no one was killed. But the only injury was to a wrangler who'd sprained her ankle dodging an excited tops. The way Frank had reconstructed the scene, Unwin had tried to create a diversion to cover the boy's escape and his own, but only the boy had made it.

Nothing could have prepared Phil for the full force of his father's anger. Alex had never struck him before; the angry red print of his open hand still burned on Phil's cheek, palpable in imagination, if not visible. And the words . . .

Tears gathered, and Phil would have let them come if Seaton had not been so cold and armored and far away in the seat beside him. Phil stared at the cloud-clotted landscape below, forcing the raw memories back. He would show no emotion. He would save it for later.

But one thing he would not let go of; he sucked on it, nursing his resentment against Alex: nothing justified Alex's hatred of the savage boy. A dead animal could be reconstructed, if not revived; nothing could replace a dead human. And nothing would resurrect a son's dead respect.

Phil leaned forward in his seat. "Frank, what's that?"

A thin track of white smoke was rising swiftly out of the dawn-shadowed forest. In an instant it had pierced the hazy cloud deck and now bent toward them in a wide smooth arc. Differential speed made the tracer smoke slide rapidly against the background of jungle and mist.

Seaton must have seen the thing even before Phil, for his reaction was too fast for thought. Already he'd pushed the control yoke hard over, and Phil suddenly found himself hanging sideways from his crash harness, staring straight down over Seaton's shoulder at the trees far below. For the briefest moment the helicopter wobbled under the unbalanced pull of vertically spinning rotors. Then it started to fall.

Phil felt the climbing missile strike, a single brutal punch from a giant rivet gun, high in the center of the fuselage.

"We're alive!" he yelled, surprised and triumphant, as if it were a game and he'd just scored a point. "It didn't explode!"

Seaton, less assured of his immortality, said nothing. The instrument panel flashed crimson, the forward rotor vibrated badly, and a loud shriek announced the escape of liquid helium and high-pressure steam from the coiled metal entrails of the stricken craft. Seaton slapped switches, opening the safety valves in the steam lines, disengaging the rotors, shutting down the magnets that contained the tiny fusion reaction.

The helicopter righted itself with a jerk, hanging suspended under two counterrotating, free-wheeling rotors. Flying as an autogyro in this inherently stable configuration, it rapidly gained forward speed. But it could not long remain aloft; each meter gained in range cost as much in altitude.

"Get on the com. Tell them we're going down," said Seaton. "And get your damned helmet on." His eyes never left the twisted landscape rising so rapidly to meet the damaged machine, which fell now as freely as a winged seed on the wind.

Leri and Meria stared in awe at the glittering speck fluttering down out of the heavens, skywriting its own obituary in billowing clouds of white vapor. Finally the sky machine disappeared from their view below the surrounding canopy of trees.

The portable rocket launcher, hardly bigger than a rifle, rested gingerly in Meria's hands. She held it away from her body, partly because the tube was still hot from the booster cartridge, partly because the thing frightened and disturbed her.

Leri looked at her. "A powerful weapon," he said, swallowing.

"Langoza told the truth in that," she replied.

"You think he didn't tell the truth in everything?"

Meria looked at him angrily.

He looked away from her, shrugging as if to adjust his rope. "Let's find the wreckage. Then we'll know."

Phil's nerves were extra-fine-tuned, and his sense of time was slowed. He watched the whole spectacle unfold in front of his as if he were watching an adventure sensie.

He savored it. He almost laughed with the pleasure of it, skimming down fast over the ridges, dodging the grasping treetops, neatly threading the winding arroyo—what wonderful skill Frank showed, how buoyant and responsive the powerless helicopter felt!

All the while he was calling on the communicator (not paying close attention, really, the view from the bubble was so thrilling): "Mayday, Mayday, this is Ranger Two, we're shot and we're going down, we're about forty klicks east-southeast of your position and going down real fast . . ."

The rocky little beach was right there in front of them, how well Frank had done it, what flying! And then a treetop came up and got in the way and there was a hell of a smash and he was jerked and bounced and pulled all around and leaves and branches were whipping at the bubble and it was squeaking and scraping and then it exploded jesus right in his face and something slapped him hard all over oh god oh god worse than Alex it stung all over his face his arms his legs ohhh SHIT!

They weren't moving anymore. "Shit, shit, shit, shit, SHIT!" he screamed, *make the awful burning go away*—he was on fire as if bitten all over by ants. He ground his teeth until they threatened to splinter in his head.

Curiously, that helped. Slowly the hurts, the thousand cuts and scrapes, all began to blend and mellow and throb together in one low purple heavy hot ache.

He'd lost his helmet. It must have popped off over his head on the first bounce, for there were cuts all over his face. He brushed his fingers lightly over his cheeks and came away with a thin film of sweat and blood. On the back of his hand he could see the intricate tracery of thread-like welts. He'd been lashed hard, but not badly sliced up.

Beside him Frank sat up quite straight, his helmet still in place, apparently unperturbed by the scourging branches.

"That was great, Frank!" Phil yelled, loud in the silence. "God, I was such a baby, screaming like that, I'm sorry, I guess it just took me by surprise, I thought we were going to make it to the beach, but you were terrific anyway, just a few more meters . . ."

Frank sat very straight, and didn't move, and said nothing.

Phil shut up. He went cold.

Then the hurt came back from inside, in a blunt bitter rush against his eyes and throat.

There was a hole in the roof, and green light filtered through to fill the metal box like an aquarium. Something warm and salty dripped onto Holder's cheek and ran into his mouth. He recognized the metallic flavor of blood. He wasn't worried, though. Scalp wound, probably—dramatic, but not serious. Worst it could do was bleed all over your eyes. . . .

He tried to sit up straight. The world was all askew. What the hell was going on? This damned airplane or whatever seemed to be tipped right over on its side, and what's more it didn't seem to be going anywhere at all. Was this a doorway under his feet? All smashed in with a tangle of splintered tree limbs and a thick mat of spicy-smelling leaves, smells like bay laurel, like that restaurant, that little Italian or Greek place, whatever it was, back on Parnassus. Made him homesick for his adopted planet; the food there had character! Damn but he was hungry, so damned hungry.

Should move soon. Didn't like that whistling sound, it was getting real loud or maybe he was just noticing it and the pitch was driving him crazy, like his wife shrieking at him, you goddamned bastard you don't care about anybody but yourself why don't you wipe that long-suffering smirk off your face, and he screamed right back at her, all right go ahead then, go on the damned liner by yourself and be damned and take the little bastard with you; and it made him want to shut her up for good.

The screeching faltered.

Have to stay rational. Don't let her pervert your reason. Except when she hits you, digs those long nails in, by god nobody can be expected to sit still for that smash her just throw her out of the way . . .

"Where am I?" he demanded, shouting to stay conscious. "Please get me out!"

He listened for a moment: nothing but a hiss now, you goddamned bastard you don't care about anybody, and then a scrape and a sob.

"Yes, I'm here, can you get me out?" Holder cried.

A face peered in at the ceiling, a face all scratched and bloody, with a big purple bruise blooming along one cheek. "T.T.?" A boy's voice.

Holder stared back, puzzled. "Can you get me out of here?" he asked eagerly. "My head . . . my head is cut. And I think my hands . . ." He tried to get a look at his hands behind his back, but he couldn't get his chin over his shoulder. "They feel like they're stuck together."

The boy was crying. "Frank's dead, T.T. I tried to wake him up. I couldn't find his heartbeat."

"I'm a doctor. If you get me to him . . ."

"And then I saw where . . . where it went through him. He's dead, T.T."

"My name is Holder, I'm a doctor . . ."

Then he remembered. He remembered being taped up for the second time that night and tossed into the chopper's cargo hold like a sack of turnips; he remembered dawn and the start of the flight, the lurch and fall, the shock of the striking missile above his head, the sickening spiral down out of the sky. He remembered a glimpse of branches whipping past outside the open door, fleeing past all blurred, and then nothing.

He stared up at the face in the opening over his head, the far door. The face was Phil's. "Frank's dead?" he asked. The boy nodded.

He'd saved that wild boy, all right. Now Frank. There was meaning in this fearful symmetry. . . .

Phil scrambled through the roof of the chopper. His legs dangled a moment, then he dropped the two meters onto the springy broken branches poking through the opposite door. Phil quickly looked Holder over, pushing with his thumb at the man's head wound. "That'll be okay when I get some 'plast on it," he said. Apparently they'd taken his knife, for he looked around and then started worrying a jagged piece of the chopper's torn aluminum skin back and forth until a plate-sized slice of it came off in his hands. He took the makeshift cleaver and sawed away at the adhesive tape that bound Holder's hands behind him. "I'm getting good at this," he muttered.

Holder kneeled, holding his hands out behind him, staring at the canted bulkhead in front of him—wondering what to say. How he'd loved Frank Seaton . . .

"Crying won't help us, T.T." Phil finished cutting Holder free.

Holder looked at the boy, saw the tear streaks still wet, freshly superimposed on a net of dried blood. But Phil spoke sternly, as if he'd forgotten all that. "Somebody shot us down on purpose. They can't be far away. We have to get away from the wreck."

"Who would want . . . ?"

"Scum smuggler, probably. I called base, but I don't know whether they heard us. The com is busted, and I don't know whether the beacon is working or not. It would take them half a day to get the other chopper up from Copeville anyway."

"Are you sure you're all in one piece?"

"I'm fine. Come on."

"What about Frank's . . . ?"

"I *thought* about it," Phil said angrily. "We'll have to come back."

Holder rose slowly, steadying himself with one hand against the panel overhead. He rubbed his wrists and flexed his knees. "I guess I'm in one piece."

"Good." Phil chinned himself on the overhead door and clambered onto the side of the wreck. He bent to give Holder a hand up. With a grunt and a scuffle Holder managed to pull himself out. He stood shakily and looked around.

The helicopter was in three pieces. The fuselage had broken behind the cockpit; it was cushioned on a smashed laurel, its belly resting against an outcropping of lichened basalt. Ruptured steam lines hissed with waning conviction as pressure bled away.

Twenty meters up the steep hillside the tail rotor mount and the stub ends of the rotor hung in a shaggy juniper.

The nose and forward rotor mount were down the hill. A shattered tree trunk protruded into the remains of the blister. Frank's torn hand was just visible through shards of plastic, thrown back against the cockpit bulkhead. Holder quickly looked away.

Down through the trees Holder could see a sunny clearing, a beach of water-worn stones in the angle of a wide rushing stream. Dizzily, Holder closed his eyes and then half fell, half jumped off the wreck.

It was a long fall. He landed heavily on the dry, gravelly slope, rolled out of control, and came up hard against an oak stump. He gasped.

He heard a thud and felt a sharp spray of grit against his cheek. "Don't do a stupid thing like that again, T.T." Phil's voice was harsh. "I can't get us out of here if you break your leg or something."

Holder opened his eyes and looked at this boy whose face was a mask of pain, anger, and concern—the boy who wanted to save his life, when all he wanted to do now was die.

"Follow me. Be careful." Phil slid and scrambled down the steep slope toward the stream. Holder followed with dull caution.

They paused at the water's edge to wash and drink deeply. The water was cold, fresh, insistently rushing. The morning sun was bright and warm, though the forest air was still cool. Holder looked up at the steep wooded ridges on either side of the river. Even this close there was no sign of the wreckage; it would be visible only from the air—or to someone who knew where to look.

"Where are we going?" he asked Phil.

"This stream leads into another, and eventually to the Gorge. From the air it was plain as a map, until we got below the ridges. Here, look at me." He patched Holder's wound with a glob of sterile 'plast, talking as he worked. "We're not far from the base camp by air, but I don't think we should try that way—way too rough. There, that should fix you. We'll have to go down to the Gorge and then home."

"That will take days. What will we eat?"

"We'll do okay, T.T. Haven't you ever tried roast tops eggs?" Phil looked at him oddly. Holder thought maybe it was an attempted smile, to cheer him up. "And I saved these," Phil said, tapping the emergency ration kits he'd clipped to his belt—from the helicopter's survival gear, each could keep a person alive for several days.

Holder grunted, weary of protest. He sat down on a rock and stared at the smooth pebbles between his shoes.

Phil sat on another boulder and unlaced his boots. "Looks more passable on the other side," he said. He tied the laces together and hung the boots around his neck. He stood and waded into the swift current.

Holder lifted his weary head and looked at the boy. The sun sparkled on the rushing waters and glittered on the leaves of the trees beyond.

Fumbling with his boot laces, he copied Phil's actions. The pebbles were sun-warm on his bare feet, but the water shocked him with cold. He walked into the stream until he was standing in the middle of it, with water swirling around his waist and his bare feet digging into fine gravel that boiled up between his toes. He had trouble standing against the current, and he had to clench his jaw until he got used to the cold ache in his ankles.

This was the first time either of them had ever stepped into this river. What sort of waters were these, that tugged them this way and that, and said, come with us?

26

The wooden spade's last load of earth fell on the mound covering the Ranger's body. Ariana stepped forward and took from her daughter a delicate bowl of incised red clay, decorated with an intricate geometric pattern in gleaming black. She sprinkled the mound with a dark mixture from the bowl. "Blood and meal feed you as you feed us, blessed," the Mother said quietly. "Rest for a cycle of cycles. Bring forth bounty on our return."

Kani stood apart from the crowd, watching her. Behind her loomed the dark mouth of the grotto. A ray of sunlight filtered through the trees to pick out her hair of straw, hair of wheat—to Kani she was the incarnation of Bounty.

She handed the empty bowl to her daughter, the Successor. Her glance swept the silent bitter crowd of villagers, who stood with their belongings bundled, already prepared to march. Kani thrilled with fear when her eyes met his.

She spoke firmly, her voice amplified by the rock arch behind her. "The call comes late, the call comes early. This cycle has been short. So be it. In a season or two even these rich gardens would have cried for rest. Rejoice with me that the Goddess has taken no son of the people."

Behind Kani he heard his uncle mutter spitefully, "Kani was called, but would not answer."

The Mother looked directly at the man. "Kani was spared by the Goddess herself. In the cycle of cycles the world changes; she has sent us this Ranger for her thanks. A mortal man, like any man of the people." The Mother turned away from the grave and walked slowly away, dismissing them all, cutting off protest before it could be expressed.

When they realized the ceremony was over most of the people shouldered their bundles and began moving quietly away. A group of men lingered near Kani. Again he heard his uncle's voice. "Next time let the Goddess spare a man with a house and a garden and a wife."

"A man who *is* a man," added another, "who won't crawl back to us stripped of his initiation."

Kani would not look at them. He kept his eyes on the fresh grave. He wanted to protest that he had submitted himself completely to the will of the Goddess, that he had given her his life. But she would not take it. The same irascible old demon had come to him where he lay bound and had hissed curses at him and hauled and shoved him and then had started throwing bolts of flame in every direction—convincing Kani that the Goddess must surely have intended him for a more dignified death at some later time.

For a night and a day he had made his way through the forest, reaching the village in the ravine at dusk. He found Langoza's machine gone, the people hastily packing, and Leri and Meria standing guard over a man's body. He recognized the dead man as the pilot of the sky machine, the one who had captured him, the one who had later been kind to him, and had saved him from the wrath of the other Rangers. Kani could not fathom the motives of the Rangers, but he felt a kinship with this one, who was dead in his place.

He stooped and took up a pinch of earth and sprinkled it on the grave.

"See what poor thanks . . ." his uncle began, taunting.

"Leave us, Kareli," said a woman's voice.

Kani looked up in fear. The warrior Meria and her brother stood in the cave, watching him. *They* had killed the Ranger. He'd heard that they had brought down the sky machine with some powerful weapon. What did they want with him?

He heard the men behind him scuttle away in fear.

Leri stepped toward him. "You were dead," he said. He and his sister had an almost furtive look about them. "You were dead and your body was in the sky machine, the Trader said."

Kani's fear left him, but he didn't know how to answer them.

"We shot at the machine to recover your husk. For the thanks," the woman insisted. "We would not have killed this creature except for you."

That made Kani angry. "You want to blame what you did on me?" he said bitterly. "Go ahead then. All the village blames me."

"No, Kani, we are the ones to blame. For listening to the Trader," said Leri. "The Mother orders us to seek your forgiveness."

"Both of us seek your forgiveness," the woman said stiffly.

"Ask *his* forgiveness," Kani said defiantly, and immediately he regretted his defiance. But the warriors made no move or sound. "Of course I forgive you," he amended. And still they did not move. "Should I say more?" he asked cautiously.

Leri cleared his throat. "The Mother said you would... uh..."

"You would teach us a lesson," Meria finished for him.

The boy looked at the two adults who stood before him like chastened children, and wondered what he could possibly teach them that they did not know better than he. "Maybe she means about the Rangers," he said quietly. "The 'demon Rangers.' They try to act like demons, maybe, but I think they are people like us." He looked at the grave of the one named Seaton. "You call him a creature. *He,* at least, was a man; that I know."

From the shrine, now denuded of its paltry relic, Ariana watched the people file out of the ravine below. She had not dared risk infecting them with panic, so she had said nothing of her convictions.

She was sure that the days of the people were near an end. Whether in a few days they would all be dead, or whether instead they would be carried into captivity, her people would no longer be free to roam the forest and to till their gardens. The world would change indeed, but not as Ariana had hoped; Langoza had seen to that.

Never before had the people killed a Ranger. She knew the Rangers would not forgive them.

She heard the steady thump of distant sky machines. She turned to look toward the east, and there, over the purple shoulder of the Mountain of Vapors, her far-seeing eyes picked out the little silver bangles hanging in the sky—three, four, six, eight of them. Never had she seen so many.

And there could be no mistake, they were coming straight on.

27

Yesterday afternoon they had been laughing together, stumbling along, giddy with fatigue, kept on their feet by the knowledge that they were no more than a day's walk from the great falls at the mouth of the Gorge. Then the sun went out. When they looked up, they saw what had been a blue sky suddenly boiling with clouds.

A strong fragrant wind descended the gorge, whipping ferns and palms, churning the swift green river to froth. Blown red sand scoured their skin, forcing their eyes shut.

Phil groped for Holder and got a fistful of his shirt sleeve, and desperately pulled him up the slippery slope.

Lightning bolts, wide, bright and terrible, exploded on the rimrock. A few fat raindrops blasted craters in the sand, but even before the rain came down hard the flood was upon them, not a wall of water but a fast-sliding jumble of chocolate milk, tossing logs and boulders before it.

Straight up they climbed, and kept on climbing, while the muddy water lapped at their boots. They found a narrow ledge, and a crevice in the rock to hook their fingers in. All night they clung to the cliff, even when the roaring winds and waters finally faltered and gurgled away, and the stars came out directly above.

They had time to talk and remember, then. They tried rehearsing the epic tale of their descent through the canyon, choosing which episodes to treat heroically (the Charge of the Bull Triceratops) and which to treat comically (Stealing the Egg-stealer's Eggs). Holder didn't bother to remind Phil that he personally wouldn't be around for the telling of the tale. That wasn't the point of the exercise, anyway. The point was to keep talking, so they wouldn't fall off the cliff while dreaming drowsily of solid ground.

The gray predawn light revealed their predicament: overhead the wall kept on going straight up for a hundred meters.

Below, the drop was sheer, ten meters or more, ending in a pile of broken basalt. To fall was to fracture a leg, or more probably a neck. But the light was no help to them in locating the finger- and toe-holds they'd found by feel in the semi-darkness, which somehow no amount of stretching and groping could find again.

They discussed their predicament, and very sensibly agreed they could not possibly go up, and could not possibly go down, and could not possibly cling to the cliff for more than a few hours. It was an opportune moment for a rescue party to happen along up the Gorge trail.

They knew there would be no rescue. They had seen no searching aircraft, had seen no aircraft at all after the squadron of helicopters that had passed over to the south on the day after the crash, and those helicopters had been on no errand of mercy. Alex must be searching in the wrong place.

Holder longed for the wings of a pteranodon. They had seen them clustered by the dozens, hanging from caves in the cliff faces like enormous bats, or wheeling and gliding on the rising currents of the afternoon.

A centipede appeared from somewhere below and undulated up the rock, climbing right over Holder's hand. Holder did not flinch; he admired and envied the multiply sure-footed creature as it rippled upward out of his sight.

Now Holder watched Phil. As he studied the boy's face, despair and determination warred in him. He *had* changed Phil's life, and for the better; he could see the evidence of it in front of him. But they would take him away from Phil, even if both of them survived.

They had stopped talking an hour ago; nevertheless Holder knew what went on behind the boy's eyes—the process was visible. A meter or so out from the base of the cliff the river swirled, thick with brown silt. No points or edges of stone broke the surface, no upwelling currents betrayed hidden presences; still, the opaque fluid could mask anything.

The dilemma was simple. Jump now, and face the likelihood of a long and agonizing death, lying broken and half drowned in shallow water. Or fall later. Only in the first choice was there any hope of life at all.

But to make that one rational decision called on resources beyond mere reason. Under Holder's absorbed gaze, Phil—his racing heart visible in the vein that throbbed on his forehead—reached that decision. He jumped.

In panic, Holder jumped after him. He would not be left alone.

They disappeared under the water. The pool was deep, unobstructed. When they bobbed up again the naked fear was on both their faces. Perhaps later they would laugh about it. Not now.

From the center of the broad brown stream Claymore and Sirich watched the distant jungle slide slowly away on either side. Palms drooped under the hot sun; crocodiles and hadrosaurs peered dully at the passing airboat. The air was thick with humidity from last night's storm. Though the craft moved sedately ahead, the breeze of its passage was warmly cloying.

Following Holder to Camp Owen Gorge had proved to be easy. He had done just what Sirich, and Unwin for that matter, had said he would. But the Camp was off limits to tourists, so beyond Waterhouse Claymore had been prepared to take to the jungle at night on all fours, face blackened and knife in hand, in the worst old sensie tradition.

In talking over the situation with Sirich, a simpler approach had suggested itself. An anonymous call to the Chief Ranger, with a few choice details about the private life of his son's tutor (selected from the real Unwin's history), might be enough by itself to dislodge Holder from the protection of the camp.

She'd placed the call (sound only, her voice hoarsely pseudo-disguised). Alex Holder had neatly trapped her: under pretext of demanding evidence, he'd asked her to describe the man she was talking about. She'd given him a description of Holder.

Moments after she switched off, the innkeeper arrived at the door of her room accompanied by an unsmiling Ranger. The Ranger stayed with her, until the airboat arrived, several hours later, to fetch her to the Camp.

At least she was heading in the right direction . . .

She looked away from the hazy riverbank, glanced speculatively at Sirich, and found Sirich looking at her with a little smile, as if to say, *No, Angelica—I could have tripped you up so many times before, if that's what I'd had in mind.*

Even the unspoken thought satisfied Claymore. Aloud, she said, "I need your advice, Clarissa."

Sirich was ready to give it. "Have you considered the

truth? Alex is a blunt, stolid fellow, if I remember him correctly, but he's not without imagination. He'll be shocked, but he'll also be eager enough to give you Holder—without a word to anyone about it."

"You want me to convince a responsible official on Darwin that reverse time travel is real?" Claymore was scandalized. "My mission is to preserve the *status quo.*"

Sirich's face wrinkled in an impish grin. "You're a much worse conservative than anyone on Darwin, Angelica."

Claymore looked away. She saw nothing to smile about; it was her own status she sought to preserve. Who was she—who was anyone—to take on the burden of all history, to manipulate and adjust here and there, to try to *improve* things. Either things must remain as they were and would become, or Claymore would become responsible for everything in her past and future—for the anonymous personality-deaths of her father and mother, for the System that had crushed them, for all the good and evil in the universe.

The hot wind brought tears to her eyes.

Holder and Phil, tattered and hungry, reached the base of the Cataracts as Persephone rose in the west. To Holder's eyes the evening star was a luminous blessing in the purple twilight. The spray and thunder of the falls was all around them, softening the outlines of the scattered mossy blocks that were the only remains of the ancient soleri that had spanned the mouth of the Gorge. The man and the boy sat in the shadow of the cliff, exhausted by their climb.

Holder looked at Phil and saw a scrawny, toughened youth, newly self-confident. Phil had brought them through alive. He was a different boy than he had been, a different boy than Holder had been. Was it enough of a difference to make a difference? Some ungenerous, niggling reluctance to let Phil be, now that he had begun to exhibit competence, would not allow Holder to admit he had as yet accomplished his aims.

They were home now. The camp itself was out of sight behind thrusting cliffs, but its warm lights were liquidly reflected from meandering ripples in the broad shining stream. There was another light on the river, moving—an airboat, by the sound—coming around the bend a kilometer downstream. Seeing the boat, Holder thought of Frank.

"They'll be happy to see us," said Phil.

Holder said nothing. Camp Owen Gorge, young Philip Holder's home, was no home to him.

"I'm sorry, T.T., I didn't think," Phil said. "Where will you go?"

"I'll find some smuggler and bribe him to take me off planet," Holder said, though the truth was that he intended to find a way to stay behind, to keep watch over Phil somehow.

"You'll never make it to Copeville on your own. Wait for me in the trees—later I'll get some food to you, maybe even the coder to the boat. They don't bother to guard it up here."

"Phil, you can't keep involving yourself in my escapes. Alex will . . ."

"I'll do what's right, no matter what Dad does to me."

"Okay," said Holder, placating him. "I guess it would be pretty stupid of me to tell you to be careful, after what . . ."

"Just shut up, T.T." Phil reached out and grabbed him around the shoulders and hugged him close.

Holder steeled himself against the nausea he knew would come. When it didn't, he tentatively put his own arm over Phil's shoulder and gave him a cautious pat. They released each other and wearily struggled to their feet. They walked in silence down the broad path to the Camp.

Away across the lush lawns, black in the deepening evening, they could see yellow lights in the house. Shadows moved inside.

A stand of monkey puzzle at the base of the cliffs marked the dividing line between the wilderness and the anomalous spot of civilization that was the camp; the conifers were dark, thick, more ancient than dinosaurs. Their prickly tentacle-like branches rubbed gently together in the cool breeze from the gorge. "You'll be safe here," Phil said.

"All right, Phil. Don't rush things, okay? You've got all night."

Phil nodded and turned away. Holder let him get a few steps ahead before he began to follow, his own footsteps muffled in the thick grass.

Phil never looked back. He skipped a step, and then he began to run. Soon he was out of sight in the shadows under the trees at the front of the house.

Holder was close enough to see into the house now. Alex and Isabel were clearly visible inside the kitchen, illuminated as if on a tiny stage. Alex was sitting at the kitchen table, looking down. Isabel crossed the room toward him, said something inaudible, and then looked away. Absently she reached out to stroke the back of his neck with a cool hand.

Holder realized with a start that Alex was crying. He'd never seen his father cry; the sight unsettled him. Big wet tears overflowed Alex's red eyes and made his cheeks gleam. Every few seconds he pushed the tears away with his blunt, spatulate fingers, but still they came. With his left hand he rubbed his forehead as if it ached, but in fact he was trying to hide his face from his wife.

Every child has shared Tom Sawyer's dream of revenge, imagining his own funeral with grim pleasure. Holder found no sweetness in this intrusion on his parents' grief, but a different greed held him: he realized, with only perfunctory shame, that he was actually jealous of Phil for the joy of the reunion ahead.

Isabel heard a noise in the front of the house, and with a word to Alex she went to investigate. Holder knew it was Phil. He stood transfixed.

Then, at the bottom of the lawn, he saw the red and green running lights of the airboat as it pulled up to the dock. He saw three shadowy figures start to climb out, silhouetted against the faint afterglow on the river. One he recognized: Mamaka.

Reluctantly he backed away from the house, deeper into the shadows. He regained the shelter of the auracarias and found a nest beneath the trees, a dry patch prickly with the fallen, scale-like needles. Cold and hunger helped him fight off sleep, but not for long. He was giddy with fatigue. He slept dreamlessly.

He woke. The wind sighed and the branches of the monkey puzzle creaked. He was very cold now, colder than at any time since the trek from the wrecked helicopter had begun.

A dark figure stood over him.

"Phil?" he asked softly.

"No, Philip. Clarissa Sirich. You must come with me right away."

28

He let the airboat drift a kilometer downstream before cutting in the engine. He drove all night at top speed, depending on the imaging radar for help in following the Marsh's broad curves. Once he almost hit a swimming corythosaur. By the time the western sky was softening with dawn he was ten kilometers below Copeville. He steered the boat in among the cypresses, threading his way slowly between silent gray sentinels until he felt the pontoons scrape bottom. He abandoned the boat and waded half a kilometer to dry land, moving cautiously to avoid quicksand.

He slept all day under flowering rhododendrons.

Alex switched off the communicator and looked at the old woman who stood across from him in the darkened study.

"Do you understand why I wanted to talk to you privately, Ranger Holder?" the woman asked.

"I don't understand anything, but I know how to follow orders. They said to give you what you want, to do what you said, and not to ask questions."

"Good. I want you to *appear* to search for the man who called himself Unwin, but I don't want you to find him. And I don't want you to give any indication to my companion that you are not doing your utmost."

"Who is that man?" Alex said angrily, disobeying the orders he'd just agreed to follow.

The old woman looked at him sympathetically, but she spoke with firmness. "You will never know. I will tell you only that he had the best of intentions toward you and your son, and that he has done you no harm."

Alex, who was a good soldier to the depths of his soul, swallowed his rebellious reply. He turned away and began organizing the phony pursuit.

Late in the afternoon Holder started hiking back toward Copeville. Whenever he heard a bushbuggy he hid. He reached Whitney's just after dark.

He sat at the far end of the counter, where he could watch Whitney, the customers, and any new arrivals as they stepped onto the porch. He ordered a bottle of Palm and a plate of Whitney's enchiladas. Whitney cooked them himself; they were surprisingly delicious. Holder gobbled them down hungrily.

He paid for the meal, but when Whitney handed him back the credit blank he didn't take it. Instead he suggested that Whitney record an additional hundred cents or so on his personal meter, and give some thought to the problem Holder would now describe to him. . . .

It was almost midnight when a black-bearded man in a flashy plastic suit sauntered in. He looked vaguely familiar to Holder, although Holder could not place him. Whitney had a few words with the man at his table, then crooked his finger at Holder. Stiffly, Holder got down from the stool he'd occupied for three hours. He approached the man's table.

"Mr. Whitney has expounded your problems to me, Mr. Unwin," the man said. "If you can negotiate, oh, say three times the commercial first class rate, I think I can help you."

"I've got credit."

"You want to sit down?"

Holder shook his head.

"Have it your way. I run a little tour business, but at the moment things are kind of—up in the air. Thought I'd take a little recreational run to Epsilon Eridani. That suit you?"

"That will be fine."

"Terrific. Let's see the color of your plastic, Unwin. By the way, my name's Langoza . . ."

"What is it this time, Jim?" See tossed her long black hair and stared impatiently at the communicator on her desk.

"I'm sorry, See, but this one is *really* strange—now she wants us to clear an Earth ship to land at Cuvier Port, something called a 'Sprint.' "

"Do it. What's so strange about that? Did you think she got here in a time machine or something?"

"I didn't finish, See. She wants the clearance filed now, but the ship won't get here for another ten years . . ."

They flew to Cuvier in Langoza's lander, which—like many in its expensive class—doubled as the command module of his yatch, the *Cormorant*. Langoza's legitimate tour business gave him a convenient cover, and when he chose he could dress as conservatively as any moderately successful small businessman, although his speech pattern betrayed him as a man who'd spent time in lompocs.

Holder played to Langoza's self-esteem and contempt for the straight world. He portrayed himself as one of those know-it-alls, ivory tower types who were really no better than any lush. The role fit Holder well.

In Cuvier they picked up two crew members, a taciturn woman named Marthe who was to be their pilot to Epsilon Eridani, and a teen-aged crewman, Jorge, who had a permanent sniffle Holder easily diagnosed as a symptom of olkane addiction. Langoza made Holder put on a white uniform too, and gave him a set of slivers identifying him as a member of *Cormorant's* crew. The forgeries were terrible; Holder had no choice but to assume Langoza had placed enough bribes to insure they would never be closely inspected.

They proceeded to the orbital port, where they hooked up the living-module and mass tanks Langoza kept berthed there. With the ship now in intersteller mode, they obtained a clearance for Darwin Station and set out to lock onto the Epseridan beam. It would take them several days to align with the beam, and thereafter a little over a month to reach the holes, under constant half-gee acceleration.

Holder spent those weeks giving the rest of his money away.

"Dealer's choice, Mr. Unwin." Langoza smirked at him; he enjoyed winning.

Holder peered blearily at the deck in front of them. A sly smile crept over his features. "Ever heard of 'baseball,' Cap'n Langoza?"

Langoza grinned wider. "A very exciting game."

Marthe and Jorge exchanged amused glances; they had ferried some prize ostriches aboard *Cormorant,* but this fellow Unwin bid fair to top them all.

"Okay. Nickel ante," said Holder, going for broke. The pot in the center lit to record his five cents, and quickly increased to twenty as the others paid. Holder had less than a hundred cents remaining in his stake, but the other player's table squares all glowed with the green that indicated four figures plus.

Holder took a long sip of his drink, a big bulb of colorless liquid. Then he clumsily shuffled the cards, real old-fashioned rectangles of printed cardboard. He'd cleverly insisted that Langoza break a fresh pack before the game, but by now he'd managed to mangle them thoroughly. Jorge, on his right, cut the deck; then Holder dealt, sending the cards slithering across the tabletop in the half-gee acceleration.

"Whoa, Mr. Unwin," Langoza protested, fumbling with his hand. "Some of us ain't quite so adept as you, you know."

Holder looked at him craftily. "So you'd like me to think, Captain."

Langoza's eyes widened in innocence, while his shipmates stifled their laughter. The three of them had thoroughly fleeced their passenger when the game was straightforward five card stud; now, in a desperate attempt to turn the tide in his favor, the drunken Unwin had proposed a game so full of wild cards it could hardly be called poker—thus multiplying their chances to cheat. The crew fully expected this to be the last hand of the night, if not of the whole voyage.

Holder thought so too.

His fumbling fingers flew, dealing cards in every direction —he had to grab at one to keep it from falling into Jorge's lap, and in so doing he knocked the boy's beer bulb into his lap.

They both grabbed for it. Holder clumsily knocked it under the table, and it took him an awkard moment to catch it and haul it back to the surface. He grinned sheepishly.

With mock suspicion Langoza suggested they should check to see that Mr. Unwin had no extra aces up his sleeve.

"I'm sorry, really I am," Holder said very sincerely, and was rewarded with a contemptuous grin from Langoza.

Jorge took a sip of the foaming liquid, licked his lips, and sipped again. He sniffled.

The players studied their cards. Langoza had the strongest hand showing, a queen and a wild card, a nine. The boy had a pair of fives. The woman had an apparently worthless miscellany, but when her turn came she bet five cents anyway. Holder guessed it was mere protocol, a prior agreement with her shipmates to help jack up the pot.

On the strength of a single nine showing Holder raised a

dime. On the second round the woman folded. Langoza met and raised. The boy sniffled. Without excusing herself the woman got up and began climbing the handholds set in the far wall, up to the lander's cockpit.

"Come on, Jorge, you going to play or not?" Langoza prodded the boy, eager for the kill; clearly he had cards in his hand to back up the strength that showed.

Jorge opened his mouth, yawned, yawned wider. His fingers relaxed and the cards slid out of his hand; his head lolled back on his shoulders and he stared open-eyed at the light on the ceiling bulkhead.

"Something's wrong, Captain!" Holder exclaimed, sounding frightened. He stood up, dropping his cards, simultaneously getting an arm under the boy's arm and across his chest, and pulling the limp body across his own. With his free hand he yanked the boy's pistol from its hip holster. "Don't call her or I'll have to shoot you both," he said to Langoza, holding the weapon steady and aiming it at his astonished face. "Now come here and take a slug of this beer. It won't hurt you. But I'll kill you if you don't."

Langoza raised his hands, but didn't move. "You fuckin' son of a bitch," he said, with something like admiration.

Holder allowed the crewman's inert body to crumple to one side, never taking his eyes from Langoza. He caught up the bulb of beer and suddenly threw it at Langoza.

Langoza grabbed it reflexively.

"Drink it," Holder snapped. He was taking a chance on the smuggler's jaundiced view of the world: any man who could outsmart him would probably be willing to kill him.

Langoza eyed the liquid, weighing his chances to escape. Apparently he concluded they weren't good. He drank.

"That's plenty," Holder said.

Langoza looked at him balefully, opened his mouth to say something, and then a vaguely worried look came over his distinguished features, his knees wobbled, and he fell slowly toward the floor.

Holder bounded across the short space between them and caught the fatal bulb of beer before it hit the padded floor. He let momentum carry him to the far side of the cabin. He peered up the ladder toward the control deck. The woman couldn't be up there long; there was really nothing for a pilot to do once a ship was locked on the beam.

Then he saw her foot descending toward the first rung.

He pushed himself back to the other side of the room to give himself an extra second. When at last her head and hands appeared below the hatch, he spoke. "Change of plans, Marthe. Let me buy you a drink."

An ordinary medicine chest, such as may be found in any soleri apartment or spaceship lavatory, becomes a veritable pharmacopeia of useful poisons to an experienced epidemiologist in need. With the means in hand, most of Holder's energy had gone into creating an opportunity to use it.

He spent a few extra minutes packing as many contraband dinosaur hides into the escape capsule as he could fit on top of the three sleeping occupants. He sealed the hatch, made his way up to the cockpit, and settled into the command couch. He reached over his head, flipped off a safety cover, and depressed the trigger that jettisoned the lifeboat. On the screen he could see it dropping away behind. Within a few days Customs would track it down by its automatic squawker; Holder didn't really care what the Rangers did with Langoza and his accomplices after that, but he hoped they might take the hint of the stolen skins.

He spoke to the control computer: "*Cormorant*, I have a problem for you. . ."

The Lorentz transformations are precise, and the passage of half a millennium had taken nothing from their usefulness. Solutions appeared on the instrument display, changing constantly as the yacht continued to accelerate. Holder stared at the equations, watching the symbols cascade past in a stream of light, while his hand rested heavily on the chrome lever that would execute the course change.

The mathematical problem, the simple problem, had been solved. Other problems remained.

"My God, Clarissa, did you follow me here? Why? How did you find me?"

"No time, Philip. You are pursued by a dire opponent."

She led me to the boat, showed me the code sliver in the lock and the clothes from my room and the food from stores. Phil's work, she claimed, but she said he'd been called away before he could rouse me. For his sake I had to be gone before he tried again, she said.

Again I asked her where she came by her omniscience,

but she ignored me. "You now," she demanded. "Where will you go?"

I saw no reason to hide the truth from the woman who had made all my efforts possible. "I'll hide in Copeville. I've got plenty of credit left, I should be able to hire a structural makeover. Somehow I'll get back here and finish the job I started."

"No, Phil, you can't take that risk now. Claymore knows everything, and the Darwin authorities are on her side. She'll track you in no time—your only chance is to get off-planet immediately."

And she told me what to do. She'd cover for me as long as she could, she said.

"What's in it for you?" I asked her. "Why do you even care?"

"We'll meet again. Then I'll tell you everything, I promise."

There were many things he would never find out if he didn't take the next step. His hand tightened on the lever and he pushed it home.

Verniers pulsed. A low warning tone buzzed. "Off the Epsilon Eridani beam," the navigation screen announced, in bright red letters.

"*Cormorant,* override the beam warning."

The warning buzzer fell silent and the blinking red light went off. Holder sighed and drummed his fingers on the arm of the control couch, unconsciously mimicking the ship's former owner.

He was committed now; he was heading into the future. Would it be any improvement over the past he was leaving behind?

Stage Three:
Darwin and environs, 186 N.E.

29

The woman whose friends called her See rubbed her fingers over her weary face and turned away from the Special Projects computer display. She felt tantalizingly close to answers she had been seeking for almost too many years to count, but even her eternally restored body could become bone weary if she insisted on mistreating it.

Better to put aside her private studies until she could resume them with her full attention; one virtue she possessed above all others was patience. The delegation from Earth was due to arrive in two days. It was essential that she devote all her time to the delicate diplomatic chores ahead.

Another appointment was imminent, although See had not discussed it with anyone. Ten years ago she had watched herself—indubitably herself, Clarissa Sirich, although disguised as a woman forty or more years older—confidently giving mysterious orders and making mysterious arrangements, the purpose of which had never been revealed. See had never questioned her alter ego, but she was convinced that when she returned, something of profound significance would be unveiled, that her self-restraint would be rewarded.

At the very least she might learn the secret of travel back in time, sometimes discussed by her scientific comrades as a theoretical possibility, but never with enough interest or conviction to result in an actual attempt. Or would to learn the method from her time-traveling self constitute an impossible paradox?

Patience! There were more immediate and pressing matters to attend to. Still, it piqued her curiosity that the landing cleaarnce Asmussen had granted a decade ago, on her orders to the strange Earth ship, the Sprint, was now to coincide so exactly with the arrival of Richard Ruiz from Earth. In a universe of possibilities, interesting coincidences were inevitable. But was this one of them?

Dawn reddened the underbellies of the clouds as the multi-wheeled tour cruiser rolled to a stop on the crest of a grassy rise. Soon the sun would rise above the cloud deck and the color would drain from the landscape, leaving only the wan yellow of the prairie grass, the hazy blue and white of the Lyell Mountains fifty kilometers away, and the sodden gray of the low clouds themselves.

But for a time the world shimmered with light, reflected from numberless ponds and bogs and from the lazy curves of the Agassiz River. Tundra grass and wildflowers were silhouetted against the shining water, like inkstrokes on copper.

The occupants of the cruiser had been traveling for half the night, en route from the Administrative Headquarters for Pleistocenia, near Cuvier. The passengers included Clarissa Sirich, Senior Research Scientist at the Institute for Biological Research in Cuvier, and her distinguished guest from Earth, Richard Ruiz, Speaker of the House of Representatives of the United States of North America.

The Speaker was an early riser, and he thought he would be the first of the cruiser's passengers to reach the observation lounge in the morning. But Sirich was there ahead of him. As he sat down she smiled and nodded.

Ruiz's helot—the only person he expected to be up before him—moved quickly up the aisle from the galley, bringing a cup of coffee. Ruiz held the coffee gingerly away from his delicate lips with a slight grimace: still too hot! This new helot was a slow learner. He glanced over at Sirich. He knew Darwinians disapproved the use of helots; though he would not hypocritically do without his servants on a state visit, he did refrain from taking disciplinary action in front of Sirich.

"I've got them," said Alex Holder, who was driving the cruiser. He had been perusing the landscape with field glasses from the vantage of the forward dome ever since bringing the vehicle to a stop. He turned toward the passengers. "Your side, Mr. Speaker. Inside that bend in the river, about ten kilometers off."

Ruiz bent forward in his armchair, pressing his face as close to the curved window as dignity would allow. The moving figures in the distance were little better than tiny black specks. He heard a commotion behind him, and turned to see his associate Macklin's puffy face pushing clumsily through the door from the sleeping area. Ruiz actively despised the pop-eyed, freckle-faced Representative from Colorado, and he was furious that the House had elevated such a crude arm-twister to a position of responsibility. But Ruiz was too shrewd a politician to make waves until he'd arranged matters a little more to his liking. Then he'd get rid of the jerk for good.

"Macklin, you bring those glasses?" Ruiz asked irritably, as if addressing a helot.

"Wha . . . ? Oh, just a moment, Richard. I'll get them." Macklin started to withdraw.

But Sirich leaned across the aisle. "Take mine, Mr. Speaker. I've seen this sort of thing often."

"Why thank you, Dr. Sirich." A perfectly charming woman, Ruiz thought. And certainly a much more important figure in Darwin's Central Council than she pretends to be.

Ruiz adjusted the collagen contacts of the little glasses as Macklin came forward to take a seat. The view outside snapped into focus, excitingly close: a band of perhaps a dozen skin-clad hunters had isolated one of the largest of a herd of mammoths. The other hairy beasts were lumbering off north across the Ice Age landscape in a fast loping shuffle, their knobby heads and small ears thrust well forward as they fled the predators. But the chosen victim, an old animal with silvery gray streaks in its brown wool, was being driven slowly and inevitably toward the cliff-like river bank.

"Most impressive!" said Ruiz enthusiastically. He seemed glued to the glasses, which hummed quietly, stabilized by a tiny high-speed flywheel. "You say they've been following the herd for several days?"

"We've been tracking the hunters for about three days now," said Alex. "That's how we figured they'd probably make the kill early this morning."

"Well worth the trip," said Ruiz. "I'm even more pleased we concluded our business early, Dr. Sirich, so we could have time for this."

"How long's this exhibit been on display?" Macklin asked, yawning. He had curled up in the seat behind Ruiz, paying little attention to what was going on outside.

"This is the first group from Cretacia," said Alex to Sirich. "The Ariana people."

"Yes. Thank you, Ranger Holder. In that case, gentlemen," she said to Macklin and Ruiz, "this group would have been in the field, oh—allowing for a couple of years of on-site training—about four or five years. Generally we'll want to observe them for at least a year to make sure they're conforming to known cultural parameters in the absence of direct supervision, before we allow visitors." She added casually, "In fact, Mr. Speaker, that would make you the first non-Darwinian to observe this particular group."

"Well, I consider that an honor," said Ruiz. "I mean it."

"You're very kind," said Sirich.

Ruiz watched the scene in rapt fascination. Nowhere on Earth could one see anything to compare with the scope and primitive grandeur of the scene. After a moment he said, "Perhaps the most amazing thing is that these people haven't been altered in any way. Is that correct, Dr. Sirich?"

"Not physically altered. In this case even the fair appearance—the pale skin, yellow hair, and so on—is quite natural. As far as we can tell these people are descendants of a small group of Darwin's original settlers—settlers of Bounty, that is—whose own ancestors were Scandinavians on Earth. Coincidentally, that makes them physically ideal for this sort of environment. But beyond mere considerations of historical accuracy, our extensive research has so far suggested no method of adjusting human neural systems without impairing vital survival mechanisms. These effects may be less obvious in a civilized setting," she said, in reference to the practice of brainburning, so widespread on Earth, "but I'm sure you can understand why the members of a tribe of hunter-gatherers need to keep all their wits about them."

"Yet somehow you've trained these people to live like barbarians," Macklin said flatly.

"In more than one way their life now is a good deal *less* barbaric than before they were reeducated," Sirich said.

"That's true," Alex Holder put in. "These people and their ancestors led a furtive existence for centuries, hiding in caves, living off nuts and berries and sweet potatoes. Finally we caught them and rounded them up. We like to think we did them a service."

"Thank you, Alex," Sirich said, retaking firm control of the narrative. "This group and many others like them underwent a long and intensive indoctrination into contemporary life on Darwin . . ."

"You call it 'indoctrination'?" Macklin interrupted. "Not

'brainburning'?" His tone insinuated the distinction was purely semantic.

"Not anything like brainburning," Sirich patiently affirmed, "just simple instruction. And after that period we gave them a straightforward choice."

"Choice of what?" Ruiz asked, not taking his eyes from the glasses. By now the hunters had driven the mammoth well into the gooseneck of land embraced by the river's swift but shallow current. The line of hunters stretched from shore to shore across the tiny peninsula. The mammoth had become aware that he was trapped.

"A choice of whether to join the mainstream of Darwinian society, or be trained further for life in Pleistocenia. In the case of this group, almost all the men and perhaps a quarter of the women chose to become hunters. Of those remaining, all of the women and most of the men have adapted well to New Era civilization."

"Remarkable," Ruiz murmured, intending a compliment.

"What about your *other* so-called 'evolutionary epochs,' Doctor?" Macklin asked, in that needling tone of his. "How do you get consenting adults to play ape-man a couple of million years lower down on the scale, huh?"

"We don't." Sirich paused briefly, then went on as calmly as before. "Our research has only recently begun to delve directly into questions of human evolution, Mr. Macklin. We have not thought it appropriate to create hominids other than *homo sap*."

The mammoth had turned now, and faced his tormentors.

"Okay, but these people here," said Macklin. "I suppose these pretend savages can always change their minds if they get tired of the Stone Age?"

"No," Sirich said coolly. "We gave them a year in the field to commit themselves. We made it clear there would be no contact with civilization after that. In fact, that's why we won't go any closer this morning."

"And if they get sick or injured?" Macklin fairly crowed. "If the game is scarce? If they're snowed in?"

"They die."

Ruiz's grip on the glasses faltered, but he'd heard her correctly. They definitely did things differently here on Darwin, where an intact mind was valued more highly than life itself. His gaze was drawn back to the life-and-death drama on the distant plain.

"Nature is harsh," he heard the woman say to Macklin, as he continued to watch. "Our purpose here is to recreate the natural history of Earth in every appropriate detail. We believe it's important to preserve a living record of the homeworld of the human race, even though our real home has long been considerably—altered." Ruiz watched the blond hunters launch a wave of spears at the cornered mammoth: their wrists snapped forward at the last instant, propelling flint-tipped projectiles from short atlatls with stunning force.

The tiny stabilizer of Ruiz's glasses hummed. Inside the comfortably warm lounge of the tour cruiser the ventilation system whispered. Ruiz held the little glasses lightly with the fingers of one hand while he reached for the coffee he'd set down on the bar tray in front of his couch—it was cool enough to drink now.

In the view from the glasses the mammoth screamed fearfully, silently. A half dozen spears hung from its bloody flanks. The terribly wounded animal staggered backwards and, seemingly in slow motion, fell from the high bank of the river, collapsing heavily onto the gray sand beach below. Though he struggled still, plainly one of the creature's legs had broken with the impact of the fall. The hunters raced to the edge of the cliff to peer down at their prey, which would provide them with meat and bone and ivory and leather and wool for months to come.

"Mr. Speaker, Dr. Sirich, sorry to break in," said Alex. "But if we're going to get you back to Cuvier in time, we'd better think about leaving."

"Can't the plane pick us up here?" said Macklin petulantly.

"Policy forbids unscheduled overflights anywhere on Darwin," said Sirich. "I'm sorry, but I'm not in a position to bend the rules."

Ruiz finally tore his gaze from the spectacle outside. "Don't fret, Doctor, you've been most kind." He leaned over the arm of his chair and returned her glasses. He gave her a long grateful look from his fine dark eyes. Then he turned to Macklin. "Get that helot to bring me some more coffee. Drinkable, this time."

30

"O Pili, Pili, how can you be so good?" Her crooning voice was as high and thin as a ten-year-old's. "You always forgive me . . ." She clutched his chest with a curled hand, all fingers, like a baby's fist clutching the breast. Outside their bedroom the sky was turning pale, and a thousand birds chirped and twittered.

Phil took her by the shoulders, tried to pull her close. "Damn it, Maya . . ." (groaning, not angry; he'd been in hell for over a year and the ache never went away) ". . . I'd never go anywhere without you, you know that—"

Her eyes seemed to film over. "You want to leave, I know it." Abruptly she pulled away from him, rolling out of the bed and onto her feet. She looked back at him over a bare bony shoulder, her eyes now full of strangely flirtatious hatred. "Don't try to change your mind now, you bastard. It's a little late to say you're sorry."

He sat up. Had it been another trap? Had she trapped him again so easily? "You damn little bitch." In that moment he hated himself more than he hated her.

She savored the obscenity; her eyes lit with triumph—it was so *sweet* when he lost control. She leaned toward him, her hands hooked, snatching at his face. He flinched, raising an arm to cover his eyes.

She cowered away as if terrified, screaming "No! Don't touch me!" in a raw high-pitched screech that set his teeth on edge. She wheeled, and her claws swooped down on the crib and caught up their son, startling him from his drowse, his pursed mouth wetly smacking as the pacifier fell away.

Phil struggled to his feet, trying to be alert and ready, though his head buzzed with distraction.

"Don't touch me! Don't you dare touch this baby!" Her lips were pulled back in a gorgon's mask; she held the wriggling discomfited child out in front of her with both hands as she staggered backwards into the corner of the little apartment, seized with an ecstasy of self-dramatization.

He knew his only recourse was to stand there numb as a post, audience and supporting cast of whatever production she had chosen to stage this morning, his only comfort the hope that if he kept his place today's scenario might not require the services of the neighbors or the police.

He stared at her pale distorted features, waiting for whatever would come next. He thought of the other times . . .

In the beginning, when he still thought the arguments were about something, something specific, he'd tried reason. She twisted each word, using it only to pump her fury higher. He redoubled his efforts to be rational; her hysteria increased logarithmically. Once she actually threw the child at him, changing her mind an instant too late, and Phil had been lucky to catch him—he thought his throat would burst with the pounding of his heart.

The next time (a week later? a day?) he thought he saw it coming again, and he tried to snatch the child away first. She'd clung to him as desperately as the false mother before the judgment of Solomon, confident she could defeat Phil by her willingness to see the baby's arm torn off before letting go.

He tried silence. He wouldn't talk to her when she started; if it got too bad he simply turned and left the apartment. Her shrieks and curses would follow him onto the street. But when the "accidental" fires began, he never dared leave her again, without her leave . . .

"Phil you bastard, listen to me! You can't stand there pretending you don't hear me—"

Her pinched harrowing features swam briefly into focus in the morning light. Then they receded into some bright sharp corner of his mind, while with the rest of his consciousness he went on mulling the impossible predicament. He realized quite clearly that she was screaming at him, that she'd already struck him once, twice, hard enough to draw blood—so hard she'd apparently twisted her hand. He felt her pain, and his own. But he was unmoved. He heard her words, but he was untouched.

He saw her hatred turn to puzzlement, her spite become mixed with fear. Did he think he could frustrate her performance—*did* he?—by the simple expedient of being present without being *here?* She'd show him something new, then. And when she had, she'd leave for Epsilon Eridani without him, just her and the baby.

He noted her remarks. He noted that some part of his mind objected strenuously, that some part of him owed love and protection to the baby, indeed to both of them, and that some part of his body yearned to move, to reach out, to block her exit. He noted all these feelings with great interest, and he did nothing.

She dressed and packed quickly. She screamed at him to help her carry the heavy bags. When he still did nothing she cursed him at length, while efficiently unpacking and repacking the essentials. Hoisting the wailing baby onto one hip, she slung a plastic satchel of the child's things over one shoulder, reaching for the remaining suitcase with her free hand.

But she paused before picking it up, straightened, looked at him with a face as pale as a banshee's. She stalked into the kitchen alcove. With one practiced hand she jammed the recycler open with a fork from the sterilizer, then shoved a length of tablecloth into the orifice—all the while clutching the child to her hip with her other arm—until black smoke started pouring from the chute.

Back to the sitting room now; as Phil watched he could read her thoughts on her face: a quick look around, smash two pictures, pull over the book shelf (leap back! Just in time—watch, don't let the baby overbalance you, he's bawling so loud now he can't catch his breath), hurl the heaviest lamp at the window (only cracked, not smashed through, shit), then grab the heavy bag and with careless superhuman strength lift it off the floor.

Out through the door, out through the crowd of gawking half-clothed titillated neighbors, out of sight.

"There's a fire in there!"

"Lord, those people . . ."

The apartment full now of bustling busy people, yanking at the burning cloth, pawing the debris.

"Good God, boy, why don't you put some clothes on? What's the *matter* with you?"

Numb but alert he stood, the tears streaming.

31

"Finally cornered you," said an eager whisper at her shoulder. Claymore wheeled to face Macklin grinning at her, his eyes bulging. "By far the most beautiful woman in the hotel, and strangely lacking in companionship. Don't deny it! I've been watching you all night—waiting for that old bag to go to bed and leave you to me."

Confusion rendered her speechless. Her instinct was to brush off an offensive pest, something she could have done almost without thinking—but it was as if she saw him in double exposure, her knowledge of who he was, or rather who he *would* be, short-circuiting her defenses.

Meanwhile he'd pressed her further into the shadows of the wisteria arbor. The soft pastel light of the paper lanterns hanging from the trees in the courtyard did not penetrate the gloom; his teeth and the whites of his huge eyes gleamed in the darkness. "What's the matter, gorgeous? Some animal got your tongue? Stinking planet crawls with them." He laughed. "Hope you're not a native."

"No," she said, pushing the words out to create space between them. "I'm from Earth." She could smell the alcohol on his breath.

"Wonderful!" he crowed. "Not Washington, though—it's a small town, I wouldn't have missed *you,* no matter how high that old fart Ruiz's had me jumping."

"I'm from New York—Mr. Macklin."

"No you don't! *Ted,* gorgeous. And you're—"

"My name is . . . Angela."

"Perfect! My angel, come to save me from death by boredom. Here, you've been nursing that one much too long." He shoved a tall glass at her.

Meekly she took the glass and sipped: rum. She hadn't drunk alcohol since she'd left the Guild, and then only on business. She grimaced.

"Throw caution to the winds," he urged. "You're with me." He took the fruit punch glass she'd been holding and tossed it into the shadows. It shattered on the flags.

Her mind raced. Somehow she had to find a way to put Macklin off. The man was no more conceivable as a sex partner than her dead father. But her head was filled only with the music drifting from the hotel ballroom. A quartet. Corelli . . .

"That's better! Take the edge off that thirst. Now tell me what's a nice girl like you, and so on."

She looked at him, allowed a smile to play over her soft lips. "Just on vacation, Ted. I happen to like animals."

"On vacation! That must be some business you're in, up there in Nuevo Yorko!"

When improvising, stay close to the truth—the first and oldest rule of lying. "You might say I'm in the personal consulting business."

He got the point. "No wonder you're loaded, Angel. I take it back about the nice girl." He gave her an appraising look. "I bet you're *good* though. So what would it cost a guy, say for . . ."

"Talk to me when we get home, Teddy." She cut him off, then let her smile turn mocking. "I told you, I'm on vacation."

He snatched the drink out of her hand, spilling half of it on her silk skirt. "Cunt. If you're not working you'll put out for free—"

"Where *have* you been, dear?" Clarissa Sirich demanded, stalking into the shadowy arbor in the manner of an enraged duenna. "And Mr. Macklin! Really, I hardly expected . . ."

Macklin snarled under his breath, pushed roughly past Sirich and stalked toward the ballroom, tossing the superfluous glass aside to crash, like the first, on the paving stones.

Claymore felt nauseous. She held her stomach while she tried to smile at Sirich. "He's hard on the glassware—"

"Macklin." Sirich watched him disappear, then turned a sardonic eye on her companion. "The survivor."

"You put him up to that!" Claymore blurted. "*You* do something about him." She allowed herself to show her strain. "You brought me here, Clarissa; do you think you're deceiving me?"

Sirich's ancient face lifted in mild surprise. "Yes. I thought I'd been deceiving you rather successfully."

Claymore recovered. "Forget it. Why should I blame you?"

"I don't blame *you* for what that man is either." Sirich shrugged. "Besides, they say people grow into office—"

"Oh, but that *is* the way he is," Claymore said with feeling. Then she was silent, biting her wet lip. "The truth. But getting rid of one son of a bitch won't change anything. They're all like that." She pulled the scarf from her neck and dabbed at the stain on her thighs.

"Too bad about the Holder baby though, isn't it?" Sirich said. "And all those others."

"Too bad Cain killed Abel," Claymore snapped. "What do you want me to do, go back and yank the apple out of Eve's mouth?"

"Interesting thought experiment—would anyone survive it? But don't misinterpret me, Angelica, I have no desire to see you change the world. Would I have given you my full cooperation if I did? Would I have arranged things so you could be wherever you wanted to be, without interference, so you could fulfill your ultra-conservative mission? I think you understand that without me you never would have gotten half this far."

"Of course I understand that. But I don't understand *why*. And I don't trust you."

"You have no reason to; perhaps I should give you one. Come with me, Angelica. Sit down with me." She took the younger woman by the arm and led her toward a small table, under the lantern-hung branches of the huge spreading banyan in the center of the court.

A waiter approached, but Claymore shook her head and he went away. Around them in the darkness couples and larger groups formed, dissolved, and reformed, all members of the goodbye soiree given by the Darwin government in honor of Richard Ruiz's visit. Human language flowed about Claymore and Sirich, as incomprehensible in source, as inevitable in force as the dumb blind élan of the twisting vines and branches. When Sirich began to speak, her voice was as rich and supple as old leather. "What would you think of someone possessed of great and powerful knowledge, Angelica, knowledge that could shake the universe to its foundations, who was willing to risk it all on a personal quirk? A quirk like honor, say, or curiosity, or a mere personal opinion . . ."

"I wouldn't know what to think. Perhaps she's a hero. Perhaps a lunatic."

"Let me tell you a story. Do you know of Evariste Galois?"

"The name doesn't mean anything."

"Early 19th century O. E.; ancient France. A student of some sort. His politics were considered radical at the time—I admit I haven't any notion of what the issues were, but I understand that most of the bright young people of his day were radicals. He was undisciplined, rude, and badly educated—this last because he refused to study what didn't interest him. Also because he was so far beyond the capacities of the best instructors in what *did* interest him that they could not follow what he was saying, and thought him stupid. Thus he learned contempt, an attitude that betrayed him, as it has many others." Sirich spoke with the assurance of one who knows. "Honest cynicism, while intellectually respectable, makes it impossible to distinguish among competing human values. Survival may be valued more highly than awareness, for example, or vice versa. Love displaces reason, or the reverse. In Galois' case, he fell in love with a prostitute."

Claymore said nothing—she'd told Sirich nothing of her past—but she felt a touch of cool pity for this fool Galois.

"Even after he found how easily her honor could be bought, he continued to defend it for the sake of his own," Sirich continued. "His political rivals took advantage of his extravagance and insulted the woman in his presence. He came to her aid and found himself challenged to a duel. He felt he had no choice but to accept, although the man who challenged him was a fell marksman."

"Perhaps I have heard this story," Claymore said. "In some other context."

"Perhaps more than once. Great legends never die—they are metaphrased," Sirich remarked. "The night before the duel, knowing he would surely be killed, Galois wrote down everything he knew of mathematics. It was his estate and his will, all in one—he had nothing of value to leave behind except his ideas. He was up all night writing—they used quill pens and ink in those days, writing was a tortuous process—and in the morning he stuffed the papers into his pockets and went off to be shot. Perhaps out of contempt, his assassin shot him badly. He didn't die until late into the night. His younger brother held him in his arms and wept for his agony. 'Don't cry,' Galois said to him. 'I need all my courage to die at twenty.' "

"Twenty years old." It was a silly romantic tale; Claymore

tried to hide her emotion. "What became of his papers?"

"Oh, nothing, for about fifteen years. Nobody could understand them. At last they came to the attention of a superior mathematician, who not only recognized their worth but had the influence to get them published. Did I mention this is a true legend?" Sirich asked. "On those scraps of paper he'd written so feverishly, Galois had sketched the foundations of the theory of groups and, virtually single-handedly, invented modern abstract algebra."

"I'm suitably impressed, Clarissa. Sincerely. But . . ."

"The connection? Like Galois, I have knowledge to shake the universe, at least the universe of thought." She smiled, but it was not a cheerful smile. "Like Galois, I lack a sense of proportion, though, unlike him, love and honor are not my vices. I have no more honor than a crocodile, a creature to which I have sometimes been compared." She leaned back, deeper into shadow. "Curiosity is my particular vice; I will go to almost any lengths to satisfy it; I will cheerfully risk my own life and the lives of any number of others to find out something I want to know. As for you, I would have betrayed you a dozen times over if it had suited my purpose. So far, at least, it has not."

"I don't believe you," Claymore said, worried, reaching out for her friend's hand.

"You are so desperate for love that you will grasp at the rankest counterfeit," said Sirich coldly, withdrawing her hand before she could be touched. "I've been able to fool you only because you want to be fooled. Your talent in the persuasive arts is at least the equal of mine, though I have a few extra years of experience. The prostitutes taught you well —naturally I know your history—they taught you the methods of widening the eye, widening the pupil of the eye, phrasing contradiction as question, phrasing command as compliment . . ."

Claymore grew aware of her surroundings with a finely tuned sensitivity that located each obstacle, each escape route, each human body within twenty meters of the table.

". . . the use of touch, the use of scent. Actors are universally distrusted because they lie with actions and words as well, a purely human achievement of which no dumb brute, trapped in the unambiguous language of behavior, has ever been capable. And you and I are far more skilled than any sensie star; to each other we should be as open books. . ."

Far from losing herself in anger or self-pity, Claymore felt as if she were emerging from a blinding fog of dull emotion.

"... yet somehow you have persuaded yourself that I care for you!" Sirich said scornfully.

Claymore weighed her chances of killing Sirich without being detected, or at least without being detained. The deed could be done easily.

"And still you cleave to this insane mission." Sirich paused to study Claymore's reaction. "For the sake of your precious status quo you will protect this narrow, selfish man, Macklin, who will fail to pursue the policies of Richard Ruiz—who is, I grant you, an equal son of a bitch, personally—and thus hasten, if just a little, the cultural collapse of your nation and your planet. Macklin, a man who will diminish the quality of billions of lives by his mere continued existence! Of course your mission is meaningless, whether you act or refrain from acting, but the self-deception you have practiced...! Not only can you not affect the history of your world, you can never even return to it."

"Why do you want to torment me?"

"Will you kill me? You can do so easily," Sirich laughed. "I'm curious about that. I also wonder if you have what makes a human as clever as an ape—do you have curiosity, too?"

Because Claymore did, she would not answer.

Sirich grinned wickedly. "I have no need of you or your beautiful space-time ship any more, Angelica. You have taken me everywhere I was curious to go. The *Griffin* will carry me on from here."

"Once I accused you of being suicidal," Claymore said, genuinely surprised. "Was I right after all?"

"The *Griffin* is destroyed, but for a few survivors. Everyone assumes all the rest are killed. I think not."

"You still think Holder will...?"

"I suggest he's dead. Perhaps the smugglers killed him. Or perhaps he only lost his nerve."

Claymore studied the woman, so very hard to see in the deep shadows. The sounds of the string quartet drifted from the hotel—Mozart now—and Sirich seemed to be smiling again: the contempt she'd mentioned earlier?

"A final word of advice," Sirich said. "You are skilled, intelligent, a superb mercenary by inclination and training. You have a marvelous piece of equipment at hand in that ship of yours. Take it. Use it. Go find a war—Brindle's a good bet, they're always fighting about something. Live like a goddess instead of a slave."

"I have a better idea," said Claymore. "I'll give you a lift up to the *Griffin*."

Sirich cocked an eyebrow. "Do *you* still believe Holder will show up? How romantic of you! Perhaps you have reason—how his Hippocratic heart must bleed for all those lost souls."

"Perhaps I've overrated Holder, Clarissa. Perhaps I should have been watching you all along."

The old woman's eroded face smiled even wider. "Indeed, Angelica, you are the equal of any ape. That's why I took a chance on you and booked *two* passages on the *Griffin*."

32

A few hours after his neighbors took him to the local clinic, Phil was released. His biochemical profile revealed he was not in violation of either the genetic laws or the controlled substances laws, and that—although mildly depressed—he constituted no danger to his own or anyone else's health or well-being. The bored psychiatric technician snapped her purple gum, gave him the pills the computer prescribed, and sent him home to rest.

Meanwhile he'd changed his mind about letting Maya go, as he knew he would (the ability to predict one's own behavior does not imply the ability to change it). Unfortunately, she'd cleaned the apartment of every negotiable moneysliver—he'd watched unprotesting as she'd rifled his pants pockets—and he could find only one half-used transitsliver in the pocket of his winter cape. But right now he needed transit more than food.

He took the levitrain to Cuvier Port. From the train's windows he watched great dirigibles, their towering gray fabric sides rendered pale blue by the distance, rising with slow dignity from their moorings on the far side of the field, bound for the distant continents of Darwin.

He waited in the tacky lobby, a collection of barely distinguishable souvenir shops, bars and restaurants, restrooms, baggage and transportation facilities, choked with vines and bushes and flowers like all the cramped dull architecture of Darwin.

On the field, orbital shuttles accelerated rapidly down the long magnetic launch rail, spread thin silver wings, and soared a thousand meters into the sky before igniting rockets and rapidly dwindling from sight. Passenger manifests were publicly displayed in the lobby facing Customs, so Phil knew Maya hadn't left the surface yet. The last shuttle for *Griffin* would leave at midnight.

He curled up on a padded plastic bench where he could keep an eye on the Customs enclosure, and half nodded off. He was glad his passage aboard *Griffin* was non-transferable; otherwise there'd be no point in his waiting to go with her, for she'd have cashed in his ticket hours ago. What kept them going through all this, time after time? His commitment to her went deeper than the obligation of support, which so far as she was concerned would expire in a few months anyway, with the end of their first triad. And he sensed that in her twisted fashion she had a commitment to him as well . . .

It was a little over six years ago that Dad was transferred to Pleistocenia—a promotion, a move up the evolutionary scale. That was the year they let those people out of Reeducation. Some of them ended up back in Dad's new territory. I hope they never realize it.

I met Maya while I was going to school in Cuvier. She was a tour guide on one of those little hovervans that take tourists around the Esplanade. It was the hair—the others who went straight had their hair and skin altered. She kept that yellow hair people stared at.

So it was easy to find out who she really was, even though the information was supposed to be strictly confidential. Dad had his own files. She was the middle daughter of Ariana's family. One disappeared; the other, the oldest, went to the reservation with the men. Their mother was killed that day . . .

Maya let me take her out a few times, she even invited me over when her friends were there, but never alone. They weren't my type, really: starving poets, would-be actors like her. She wanted to be in the sensies; I thought that was cute but sad. There was that one very nervous psychiatry student who was the drug source, I think, and those junior-exec Rangers who were chasing her "primitive" body. Maya's Minions, that's how I thought of the whole motley crew. She never admitted me to the inner circle until somehow she found out who Dad was . . .

Then all those years I didn't see her, off at Esperidan; me scared to say boo in a world richer than I'd ever imagined; meeting Unwin, the real T.T. Unwin; and then a favorable alignment making it cheap enough to come home for a visit.

I still don't remember just how it happened. There was the sex, of course. The way I was raised, I thought it was strictly for animals—that's the Darwinian utilitarian cant of Biology with a capital B, as bad as Old Era Christianity for creating guilt, and without Christianity's utility in providing convenient swear words. Like all proper little Darwinians, I wasn't sure where to draw the line between humans and animals, but I was sure as hell anxious to maintain the distinction. Maya didn't see things that way, despite Re-ed. She made me feel perfectly beastly.

There was another distinction I wanted to make, that between myself and Dad. Marrying her was a way of making up for what he did, maybe. But I wonder what she had in mind when she married the son of her mother's murderer? Maybe that's another distinction she doesn't draw . . .

The marriage was secret for about a month. I have to laugh—her acting so domestic for me during the week, me acting such a loyal son when I went home to the folks on the weekends. I remember feeling pretty independent for a while back when I was thirteen or fourteen; but that revolt withered somewhere along the way, for lack of encouragement.

We had to tell everybody when we found out she was pregnant. You don't get an abortion on Darwin, unless you can prove the child wouldn't survive on its own. I was always surprised by how fast that happened—birth control is certainly not illegal. I think now it must have been the first night she was sure I was going to marry her.

The folks were so good about it I couldn't believe it. Maybe they thought it was some kind of deserved punishment—no, that's the way I looked at it. Maybe they just wanted to give us the best start in a shaky situation. They sent us both back to Epseridan.

Then Kenny was born and the fights started . . .

He woke up when the limousine from the Burton arrived outside the terminal, stopped its engines with a sigh, spread its rubber skirts and kneeled to the curb. The doors opened and a crowd of spoiled, intoxicated children of wealth swirled into the terminal. And there was Maya in the midst of them, her baby asleep on her shoulder.

Phil stood up, grasping his suitcase. He watched unnoticed as she swept past him, a tall, thin, ghostly blonde among dark strangers. He stumbled along in the train of happy passengers, keeping Maya's bobbing golden head in sight as they approached the Customs barrier. She showed her ticket and identification to the machine and swept through the gate without delay. In a moment she was outside the outer doors on the concrete, stepping into the little electric trolley that would carry the passengers to the shuttle The shuttle's slender silver hull sat poised at the end of the catapult, bathed in yellow light.

Phil stopped, ignoring a man who bumped him from behind and cursed him indignantly. Lightheaded with hunger and fatigue, he staggered to the rail surrounding the Customs enclosure and watched the others push through the gate.

He realized, with a certainty that made him want to weep, that what he truly desired at this moment, more than anything else in the universe, was for Maya simply and finally to disappear out of his life.

But then an old memory rose unbidden in front of his eyes, the face of a man he'd known once, briefly; a man who claimed to be no one at all; a man who'd tried to change his life in ways he only vaguely understood to this day. He knew the man would be disappointed with him, angry at him—angry that having come so close he had failed to act.

He pulled out his ticket and rejoined the line.

When he got in the tram Maya looked at him contemptuously. "I wondered if you'd have the guts to show up." She gave the sleepy baby to him.

They rode in silence to the shuttle. Other passengers exclaimed and pointed when a great black sleek ship with Earth markings rose in a fountain of golden fire from the far side of the field. "The Sprint," they said, excited. The mysterious craft had been a subject of much speculation since its arrival several days ago.

But Phil and Maya said nothing.

33

Follow a beam of light drawn up across the stars, bright as a molten wire; find its source in the reaction chamber of Griffin.

The thin, clean beam derives from fused hydrogen, and the liner, now a week out of Darwin, accelerates under fusion power because it is inside the statutory "life zone" around Darwin's Star. That condition will soon end.

Above the reaction chamber and its ordinary hydrogen tanks stand two vastly greater cylindrical mass tanks, many hundreds of meters tall, woven together by an intricate tangle of plumbing. One tank contains meson-superhydrogen, the other baryon-superhydrogen. A superhydrogen reaction is roughly ten thousand times more powerful than the fission of a comparable mass of plutonium, and very dirty. When the heavy quarks in the nucleons of one gas annihilate with their antiquarks in the nucleons of the other gas, all hell breaks loose.

High atop the enormous superhydrogen tanks perch the liner's comparatively tiny passenger decks, stacked like saucers: housekeeping sections below; cabins in the middle; dining salon, ballroom, and promenade deck next; and on the top of the stack, the recreation deck, with swimming pool, bars, gymnasium, galleries and lounges, all roofed with tinted crystal.

A hangar deck, little better than a tangle of mesh platforms and catwalks, gives access through tubular airlocks to a cluster of landing craft ringing the ship, including private yachts in tow.

The bulbous command-and-control module, bristling with

sensor and transmitter antennas and shield-field generators, surmounts all.

To those antennas your message is aimed. Key the demand frequency . . .

"Ladies and gentlemen, if I may have your attention for just a moment—" The white-haired, craggy captain stood on a shaded portico flanked by Grecian urns, overlooking an arm of the sea rather too blue to be called wine-dark. In the distance, rocky heights glowed cantaloupe pink in the rays of a setting sun: the entire scene was a mural in the style of the old master Parrish.

The audience glittered with jewels and ribbons; perfume and power mingled in the close air of the elegant salon.

"We'll be lighting up our beam in, oh, an hour from now or thereabouts, pushing off into deep space, and I'll have to be leaving you then to look after things," said the captain, "so I did want to take this opportunity to express how deeply honored all of us on the staff of *Griffin* feel to have aboard our vessel the congressional delegation from the United States of North America, Earth, led by Speaker Ruiz—"

The captain paused to allow polite applause. He smiled at Ruiz, one commander to another. The tall, graying man with the oddly delicate mouth nodded back.

"And we're equally honored to have with us the Republic of Darwin's trade and cultural mission, led by Dr. Sirich." He bowed in the young Sirich's direction, while the guests applauded the woman with the clear dark eyes and the frank appraising stare. "And before my throat runs dry, I'll join our eminent guests for a spot of celebration."

The captain stepped nimbly off the dais and took a bulb of what appeared to be brandy, actually tea, from the rack held out by a steward who had appeared on cue. The captain moved through the crowd, chatting affably. Considering the volatile nature of his passenger manifest, keeping everyone friendly on this cruise was almost as important as keeping the ship functioning smoothly.

Phil Holder tugged at the uncomfortable formal scarf around his throat, and gazed moodily at his wife. Blonde and several centimeters taller than the norm, Maya could not be missed in the crowd of typically dark-complexioned partygoers. Her appearance betrayed her origin to the Darwinians on board, and made her the object of attention and comment to the others. He cursed the ill luck that had booked them on the same ship to Epsilon Eridani with this collection of the powerful and famous.

Now her blonde head was plowing through the dark sea in his direction, and he assumed she'd completed her mission of having their infant son kissed by the American Speaker—a scene he'd refused to witness. When embarked on social mountaineering, Maya's dialogue was just too cloying to bear.

"Here, do something about your son," she said, her voice hoarse from smoke and chatter. She thrust the blanketed bundle in his direction. "Smell that? He would have to shit just as Ruiz was about to come our way."

"You'll have other chances," said Phil, taking the sleepy, grumpy boy. "Ready to call it a night?"

"Take care of him, I said." She turned her thin nervous features away, scanning the crowd with little jerks of her head.

"Maya, will you please . . ." But she was already leaving, the skirts of her shiny translucent maroon gown switching about her legs. Phil jiggled the boy on his shoulder, turned, and went into the central corridor toward the elevator shafts.

Richard Ruiz was exchanging some small talk with the *Griffin's* captain when a junior officer pushed her way through the crowd and whispered something in the captain's ear. He turned to Ruiz with an expression of regret. "I'm told Darwin has raised us on the radio with some news I should hear. Damned inconvenient, but they pay no attention to the time we're keeping."

"Please, don't be concerned on my account," said Ruiz.

"Good of you. I'll be back shortly." The captain headed immediately for the central lift tubes, not rushing, but wasting no time.

It was clear to Ruiz that something important had come up; he was sure he would hear about it if and when he needed to—he had complete faith in the captain's judgment. Ruiz congratulated himself once again on his perspicacity in choosing the neutral Cetian liner to ferry him and his delegation on their sensitive mission to the major planets of the Archipelago. The ship was old, but it had a certain grace the newer ships lacked, reflected in its small but tastefully appointed rooms, done in polished wood and brushed metals and roughly textured fabrics. The *Griffin* somehow managed to convey a reassuring sense of steady permanence.

That was just the image Ruiz himself hoped to convey. Despite its tribulations, Earth was still the most powerful planet in the Starry Archipelago, and the USNA could still claim to be the most powerful nation on Earth. But if diplomatic ties with other planets were not constantly and carefully maintained, the situation could easily deteriorate. He was grateful that the Darwin group appeared ready to give him solid support.

He eyed the woman, Sirich, who headed their delegation. He was certain she was a much more important figure in Darwin's Central Council than she pretended to be, despite her anomalous youth—barely forty, he'd guess. But it was always tricky guessing where the real power lay in these nations with democratic pretensions. Sirich turned and looked at Ruiz then, and smiled. He raised his bulb in her direction. He excused himself from the man who'd been talking steadily at him—he hadn't heard a single word—and made his way toward her.

Angelica Claymore stalked the edges of the crowd, the white silk of her loose trousers and jacket whispering against her limbs. She was tense with anticipation. If she'd been accurately briefed, matters should come to a head within the hour. And old Sirich should know—she'd been here before.

Claymore found her fascinated gaze drawn once again to the youngish woman talking to Ruiz. She seemed no more than a decade older than Claymore herself, with long black hair just beginning to show streaks of silver: a woman who held a high but mysterious position in the government of Darwin. *Clarissa Sirich.*

The official files she'd read on the *Griffin* disaster made no mention of Clarissa Sirich. But those were the files available on Earth; there'd been no time for her to get the complete records of the inquiry from Tau Ceti. She'd been surprised at the time at how very sketchy the records were—not even a passenger manifest—given that the wreck of the *Griffin* was a pivotal event in recent USNA history. She suspected now that Macklin had arranged matters to prevent anyone from contradicting his self-serving memories of the heroic acts he'd performed during the ship's dying moments.

Macklin—the man for whom she'd traversed the years and the light-years: there he was, in the corner by the portable bar, making a determined pass at Maya Holder. Or perhaps it was the other way around? To Claymore's eye the batting lashes and the twitching rump in the see-through maroon dress were contemptibly obvious, but then Macklin was not a man to appreciate subtlety.

Now the two of them had moved to the foot of the winding stair that led up to the galleries and lounges above, on the top passenger deck. That deck was dark and practically deserted, with most of the passengers amusing themselves here in the salon. Macklin whispered something and Maya laughed, and then his fingers brushed the point of her hip, and they were moving casually up the stairs to the dark gallery above—no doubt to catch the view.

Claymore started worrying about how Maya was going to keep her appointment to blow up the ship. Only a few minutes remained.

Someone tapped at the door of the cabin. Phil crossed the cramped little room in a couple of steps and opened the door a crack: it was Naomi, the wife of one of the junior Rangers on the mission. "I'm putting my two to bed now, Phil," she whispered. "If you want to patch your vidcom into our room I'll be happy to keep an eye on Kenny for you."

"I don't know if I'm really in a party mood, Naomi."

"Oh, go on. You might have some fun."

He thought about it; the baby would certainly be safe with Naomi keeping watch. "Well, if you're sure it's not . . ."

"Hush. Go find your wife."

"Thanks a lot, Naomi. See you later."

He closed the door. He recovered the formal scarf he'd taken off, wrapped it around his neck again, and then keyed in the vidcom. He waved his fingers at Naomi in the screen as she entered her cabin with her youngsters in tow, and he saw her wave back.

He went into the corridor, and turned to pull the door closed; he lingered a moment, taking a last peek at his son in the webbing crib—the boy was fast asleep on his stomach, his lips formed into a tiny bow, his legs curled under him and diapered bottom pushed high into the air.

Phil gently clicked the door shut.

34

The lift door slid open. Phil followed the circular corridor around to the salon.

Even more people had joined the party since he'd left it. Stewards were busy circulating with racks of drink and food. Dignity had begun to crumble; one man was being sick in an urn. Couples were drifting upstairs to the darkened galleries above. Maya was nowhere to be seen.

That worried Phil more than it irritated him; he clung to his responsibility. He turned, shouldered his way past a drunken laughing woman, and started for the stairs. He would look for her in the upper public rooms before asking questions.

An officer approached him. "Are you Mr. Philip Holder?" she asked.

"Yes. What's the trouble?"

"Mr. Holder, I've been asked to take you to the bridge."

"Is it my wife?"

"Please follow me, sir."

It was dark on the circular bridge of the *Griffin,* so dark that the numerous officers and crewpeople were only silhouettes against the stars, which were visible through the unshielded slit windows that encircled the deck. The only lights were the blinking sapphire and amber and ruby patterns on the instrument panels. The captain was bending over a communications console talking to two of his staff; he straightened and came forward when Phil was led on deck.

"Please forgive this intrusion, Mr. Holder. Will you sit down, please?" He caught Phil's shoulder and guided him firmly to a swivel chair. Phil sat, but the captain didn't. "I'm going to have to ask you some rather personal questions," the captain said. "I do so for the most pressing reasons. Your cooperation is of the utmost importance."

"Is my wife all right?"

The captain turned to an aide; Phil noted he wore a side-arm with the holster unsnapped. The man nodded.

"She's perfectly all right, Mr. Holder." The captain drew himself up a little straighter. "Now I must inform you that the *Griffin* entered deep space approximately ten-to-the-third seconds ago, and we are therefore operating under international rules, upon which I base my authority as absolute commander of this ship. Do you understand?"

"I'll be glad to cooperate if you'll tell me the problem."

"When we're done I'll tell you all I can." The captain studied the tips of his polished brown boots. "Mr. Holder, have you recently noticed any, um, strange behavior on the part of your wife?"

. . . they sent us both back to Epseridan. Then Kenny was born and the fights started, and I started practically living in the library. People started giving me weird looks. I heard her on the vidphone one night, she didn't hear me come in, and she was talking about how much I drank and how I'd get high on olkane and beat the shit out of her and slap the kid . . .

"Mr. Holder?"

"I would say yes, Captain. We've had some strictly personal problems for the past few months."

And I started doing it, too. Not olkane; who can afford it? And not Kenny—but I've been getting pretty boozed lately. Twice I've hit her, raised purple bruises on her fragile white jaw . . .

". . . I should add, if I'm going to be perfectly honest, that I've been doing some heavy drinking, which I'm sure has contributed to our difficulties." He spoke as if he were dictating a confession.

"Believe me, Mr. Holder, these questions are as painful for me to ask as they are for you to answer." The captain sounded genuinely distressed. "Tell me this, has your wife ever been diagnosed as emotionally impaired?"

I never told her about Unwin. He never liked me much, anyway, and he wouldn't say anything about the past except that once—"So you're the chap that fellow was so anxious to meet"—but I pushed some kind of forlorn displaced affection on him, for the sake of the other, and finally that morning I tracked him down and spilled a year's worth of woe right in his coffee . . .

"No, Captain, she's never been professionally diagnosed."

. . . and he just stared at me and said she was obviously crazy, paranoid schizophrenia, probably, one of the simplest of organic problems, so why didn't I just take her around to the infirmary and get her fixed up?

"And your personal opinion, Mr. Holder? Please understand this is in the strictest confidence."

I never met a "crazy" person. And on Darwin they don't mess with people's chemistry. And Unwin doesn't like women anyway, he'd say anything . . .

"We have our private disagreements, as I said. Sometimes they get a bit melodramatic. Basically I think she's, uh, socially responsible."

. . . and besides, she's got so many excuses, even my own behavior, and yes, she's completely mad.

"All right then, Mr. Holder. Finally, will you describe your current plans, yours and your wife's? Precisely, I mean what are you doing on the *Griffin?*"

I finished the B.S. with honors, maybe because they give points for agony. I was supposed to go on in biochemistry, but I ran out of will and energy. I quit. We all went home—I can't believe that was just four months ago! We ended up in that same little apartment of hers and I got a job counting chromosomes at the Institute and her creepy friends started coming around. But this time I think she found them just as pretentious and parochial as I did, mere apes of the trend setters in Epsilon Eridani. That's where she wanted to be, in the center of the universe. . . .

She knew what I wanted to do, but I wouldn't tell Dad.

Hadn't the folks done enough? I didn't really give a damn about animals. I was interested in people. So she told Dad what I didn't dare to. And Mom and Dad came through again.

"I'm going back to medical school, Captain. That's about all there is to it."

The captain looked at his aides, who were dark shapes towering above Phil in the whispering, blinking gloom. No one moved. At last the captain said, "Only one or two more questions, Mr. Holder. Come with me, please."

He led Phil to a communications console. He patted the console operator on the shoulder in a fatherly way, and the young man touched some keys. The screen lighted: a man's head and shoulders formed.

"Mr. Holder, this man claims he has evidence that your wife is going to destroy this vessel. Do you know why anyone would say such a thing?"

Phil could only stare. *Ten years, and he's aged hardly a day . . .*

"Mr. Holder, do you have any idea who this man is? Or why he would claim to be *you?*"

So little of his proper time had passed since Holder had stolen that lander from *Humboldt*. In the interim the years, the very decades, had flowed around him like a mountain stream, falling in abrupt cascades or lying still in quiet pools, but never ceasing to flow.

Most space travelers took whatever measures they could to avoid becoming victims of the twin paradox. Not Holder. The mechanics of time travel into the future had been thoroughly understood since the days of Einstein's lagging clocks and shrinking rods; the Lorentz transformations are not only precise, but relentless.

Cormorant had looped Darwin Station at a substantial fraction of light speed and had dived straight back toward the planet's orbit. The immense gravity of the two holes accelerated the craft on the approach and slowed it on the return, but when *Cormorant* crossed Darwin's orbit the planet was on the other side of its sun—a celestial-mechanical oversight in Holder's programming instructions that nearly proved fatal.

Furiously calculating the intervals between all useful sets of space-time events known to him, Holder at last ordered

Cormorant to expend most of its precious remaining super-hydrogens decelerating inward toward Darwin's star, swooping close to that fiery sun to cut across Darwin's orbit. If he had correctly estimated the delta-v's, *Cormorant* should overtake *Griffin* at a roughly matching velocity when the liner was less than a week out on its own journey to Darwin Station. That was cutting it almost too close to call, but it was the best he could do.

Once made, the decision was irrevocable. Three weeks later, Holder could just make out the indistinct speck that was *Griffin*, swamped against a glittering starry background, through the unshielded windows in *Cormorant's* nose. On the viewscreen the liner appeared close, but Holder knew he still had a long way to go. Weeks ago he'd jettisoned the dead mass of the living module and tanks, and the fuel in the lander had dwindled away to almost nothing. But he had to keep accelerating until he caught the *Griffin*, or become derelict.

The communicator screen glittered, and the lights coagulated into the image of *Griffin's* captain. "*Cormorant*, we have Mr. Philip Holder on the bridge. He tells us he has no reason to suspect his wife of planning to cause problems. He also tells us that he recognizes you, but that he has no idea why you are using his name—except that you seem to have a penchant for borrowed names. For what it's worth, he says that even though he doesn't know who you are he trusts your intentions."

"That's an honest answer, Captain," Holder said.

"I'm in no position to judge, *Cormorant*."

"What have you decided, Captain? I'm running . . ."

"Yes, you're running very low, *Cormorant*. Your telemetry tells us that. Nevertheless you're currently on the optimum heading for a rendezvous, so neither time nor fuel is being wasted. You understand I'm operating under international law, which does not require me to alter my course to rescue you if, in my considered opinion, doing so would endanger my passengers. Frankly, I haven't made up my mind yet."

"Captain, isn't there anything I can say . . .?"

"I've already told you the problems your story creates—quite aside from this reverse time-travel business, which I must simply discount. Though I'm honestly doing my best not to hold it against you."

"How good of you."

"And I don't blame you for being upset. But so far as we

know there is no way, no way whatsoever, that this woman could do severe damage to this ship without a sizeable bomb. We're doing a rescan of all areas accessible to passengers, but frankly it's a ridiculous proposition."

Holder was frustrated by his inability to answer the captain's eminently reasonable objections—he'd never figured out how Maya had done it, either. But he had no doubt she had. He could never forget the explosions that had wracked *Griffin,* the inferno that had greeted him when he'd pulled open the door of their cabin . . . The hellish vision had lived with him for twenty years.

Maya had not survived to tell anyone how she'd pulled it off. There seemed to be nothing anyone could do to interfere with the functioning of an annihilator from inside a second class cabin almost a kilometer away from it.

"Unless, *Cormorant,*" the captain was saying, "*you* are carrying the bomb."

Holder froze. "I'll jettison my ship," he said immediately.

"You're willing to come across on a line?" the captain asked.

Holder nodded.

"You understand we wouldn't stop accelerating. Once you got on that line you'd be falling toward our stern. We'd bring you in as fast as we could, but if your ship burned out before we got you across . . ."

"I'll take the risk."

The officer hesitated. Then he said, "All right. We'll transmit final approach vectors to your machine. Be warned, *Cormorant,* if you vary from them by one degree we'll torpedo you without query."

"If I may make one suggestion at this time . . ." Holder fought to keep his voice calm. "I urge you to allow Mr. Holder to join his wife immediately. And have him stay with her."

"He's already made the same request, *Cormorant.* He's on the way. Under guard."

35

Macklin's hand rubbed Maya's arm with dull insistence.

"That's a very bold suggestion, Mr. Macklin," she said; she left the arm lying there across the back of the couch, neither encouraging nor discouraging him.

"I told you to call me Ted. And I noticed you're not running away."

She studied him over the bulb of brandy fluff he'd brought to her.

"I also noticed nobody seems to be looking for you too hard," Macklin went on, "so don't tell me you're going to be missed." Earlier, on the way up the stairs, she'd casually moved a breast against his arm, a hip against his thigh, but she'd stiffened once they'd settled on the couch. "Come on, baby, relax a little," he coaxed.

Great curving windows of crystal opened onto the star-dusted universe, only a few meters in front of their couch. Couples in silhouette passed restlessly to and fro, stirred as if by invisible winds. The only light came from the burning amber eye of a beacon on the hangar deck overhead, shining through the roof plates; Darwin's Star, the nearest sun, was below the ship and on the other side.

Angelica Claymore quietly threaded her way among the thickly upholstered couches and lounge chairs, taking care not to disturb their occupants. She gleamed pale as a ghost in her rippling silks. She had come to insure that Maya Holder was not being detained against her will.

In the yellow gloom Maya smiled, allowing a hint of tears to moisten her eye. "I haven't really relaxed . . . in such a long time." She leaned toward Macklin.

His grin broadened, his eyes and teeth gleamed.

Two men appeared in the doorway at the far end of the room, silhouetted against the corridor light. "Maya?" Phil asked. "Are you in here?" There was no response. "Maya?"

A low chorus of hisses and groans greeted him from the shadows. Undeterred, he walked into the dark room, peering here and there, searching for her thick blonde hair.

"Shit," Maya whispered. "Here comes Phil."

"Oh?" said Macklin, his voice rising a note. He leaned away from her. "Well—maybe I should give you two time to get things straightened out between you."

"Sure you should," she said with disgust. "Lover."

Claymore silently doubled back. She was convinced now that something had gone wrong. The guard with Phil couldn't possibly have been a part of the original equation. Time was short; she must take care of the immediate problems immediately, and figure out the rest later.

She stepped up behind the guard, snaked one arm around his throat while the other hand covered his nose and mouth. But she had to stand on tiptoe, and almost lost him—he made one muffled, strenuous "mmmphh" that brought an amused feminine giggle from a nearby couch, but no other reaction. Claymore took him to the floor sideways, out of the light from the corridor.

She rose over the unconscious body, then moved rapidly along the wall, keeping Phil in sight.

Phil approached the couch that faced the curving windows. Two people were outlined against the stars; the woman was blonde. The man suddenly stood up, before Phil had said anything. The man tugged at his scarf, looked sideways at Phil as if considering speaking, then changed his mind and walked stiffly away, taking the corridor to the spiral stairs.

"Maya," Phil said to the seated woman.

"Shit," she said in a dry croak. "You are really bright, do you know that? Do you know who that man was? Do you know what he could have done for your career . . .?"

"I'm a student this month, remember?" he cut in, exasperated.

". . . and you had to embarrass the man in front of everyone. Now he'll . . ."

"Will you people shut up?" said a woman's voice from the shadows.

"Yeah, go argue somewhere else," a man put in.

"Come on, Maya, let's go," Phil said nervously, knowing that the situation was rapidly developing into a one-woman show.

"Teach her a lesson," a drunken man mumbled.

"To hell with you, Herb," said a woman.

Maya stood, her golden hair reflecting the amber beacon overhead, her shadowed face seemingly helmeted in glowing bronze. "This is the end for you, Philip Holder . . ."

"What the hell's that?" the drunk exclaimed. Murmuring voices and rustling clothes filled the quiet dark with sibilance, as people rose from their couches and flocked like starlings to the curving windows.

A burnished yacht swept across the stars, its gleaming black skin reflecting the full force of the invisible sun. With tiny explosions of ice crystals its verniers aligned it vertically with respect to *Griffin,* and even as it began to slide astern its main fusion engine fired with a steadily pulsing yellow flame. Its position stabilized, and it kept pace with *Griffin,* almost a kilometer distant.

"Somebody late to catch the ship?" a woman said. She giggled.

"That lander's got no tanks, no life module, not even a lifeboat," said a man. "It must be in some kind of trouble."

"Damn it!" Maya said, and no one paid her the slightest attention. She balled her fists and stalked the length of the room toward the central elevators, her angry strides punctuated by the switching of her dress.

At that moment the captain's voice came over the public address system, speaking softly from every corner of the room. "Ladies and gentlemen, *Griffin* is extending aid to a distressed spacecraft. We have made no adjustment to our flight plan, and none will be necessary."

Phil, distracted, watched for a moment as a line, thin as spider silk, uncoiled from the hangar deck overhead and arced toward the yacht. But even before the captain stopped speaking he turned and followed Maya toward the elevators.

"This is a routine exercise and it will have no effect on our itinerary, I want to emphasize that," said the captain. "We'll pass on further details as they are available."

Claymore watched Phil go, saw him pause in the corridor for a moment, puzzled, looking for his escort, but then move on. Perhaps he assumed the guard had been called away. Claymore stood still, undecided. She was used to acting on less than complete information, sensing what action to take and taking it; people who waited to act until they thoroughly understood a problem were always too late to solve it. But never had her data been so fragmentary. Why had Phil brought that guard? Should she go after Phil now?

And this ship in trouble . . .

She cursed herself for a distracted idiot, as the truth began to dawn. She stepped close to the gallery windows, shouldering others aside.

She was in time to see the hatch in the distant lander crack open, with a miniature snowstorm of frozen moisture rushing out of the airlock, the crystals falling away as straight and fast as feathers in an evacuated bell jar. A tiny figure in a white pressure suit appeared in the hatchway and fumbled with the lifeline. The line itself was invisible.

"Why is that ship so far away?" a woman asked.

At first, no one could answer her. Finally a man suggested, "Maybe they don't want to risk a collision."

"Sure doesn't make it easy on the guy. If it is a guy."

The little figure suddenly fell from the hatch. The onlookers gasped. "Oh God," a woman said, "they lost him."

But though the white figure fell steeply away, so that the spectators had to crowd against the windows to follow the fall, it was immediately apparent that the falling body followed a catenary, the natural drape of the invisible lifeline in the constant acceleration. In a few seconds the gleaming speck had reached a point midway between the ships, where it slowed abruptly, stopped, and rebounded. The figure made frantic swimming motions. "He's trying to catch the line farther up," someone said.

"Are they going to make him climb it himself? Why don't they pull him in?"

"Be patient."

The thin shining portion of the line they could see hanging from the landing deck overhead now tautened perceptibly. Below them the figure in the pressure suit was drawn slowly toward them. As the seconds crept past it came nearer and higher; the spectators peered to see the identity of the rescued pilot.

Everyone had forgotten the abandoned yacht. Tiny compared to *Griffin,* it was nevertheless sufficiently massive to hold steady under the jerking and bobbing of one diminutive human. But suddenly its steadfast rocket exhaust faltered, and the engine soundlessly belched an enormous blossom of orange flames that sent lurid shadows billowing through the view gallery. Without looking back the man on the line started pulling himself hand over hand, as fast as he could move in the bulky suit.

"Jesus," someone said. There was another soundless burst of light. "He'll never make it."

The lander wobbled and the flame of its engine snuffed out, leaving angry blue-black afterimages on the retinas of the blinded watchers. Almost at the same moment a searing bolt of white light streaked into the lander from overhead and the yacht vanished in a perfect oblate fireball—of which the onlookers saw only the embryonic beginnings, for the gallery's self-shielding windows opaqued instantly and the view outside the *Griffin* was cut off.

"They torpedoed it," a man said quietly, awed.

"They must have killed him," said a woman.

"No," said another, "they were trying to save him, I think. Cut through the line before it snapped and jerked him away."

"I wonder if . . ."

They were interrupted by a woman's loud strong voice calling from the central corridor. "Is Maya Holder in this room?" Luminous ceiling strips brightened. The room's disheveled occupants blinked sheepishly at each other. "Maya Holder," the woman repeated, imperiously. She was a uniformed guard. "Mrs. Philip Hol . . . God, what happened here?" She'd found the inert guard at her feet.

Claymore's hand moved behind her back and under her loose top, to rest on the butt of the little stunner, tucked into her waistband over her spine.

Then the crystal windows dissolved to transparency. The pilot of the vaporized lander was hanging immediately below the gallery, twisting in a loop of cable, slowly being pulled to the hangar deck above.

"No one in this room will move until I say so," the guard ordered. She aimed a firegun nervously in their direction. "Hands in the air, all of you, right now."

Claymore ignored her, staring with fascination at the body outside the windows. Slowly, slowly it swung around as it rose, until finally the face came into view through the helmet plate.

Not two meters away was Phil Holder, very much alive.

Claymore drew her gun, turned, and shot the guard.

Phil heard the pleading voice before he came around the curve in the corridor. He discovered Naomi alternately banging on the cabin door and tugging on its handle. "Maya, let me in, honey, before you do something to hurt yourself. Please Maya."

"What's going on?" he demanded.

"Phil, thank God," said Naomi. Her relief was mixed with fright. "She came in and started tearing the place apart, ripping up all your clothes, pulling the sheets off the bunk—she's acting *crazy!* She's stuffing everything down the recycler!"

"Maya, damn it, come out of there or I'm calling an officer!" He kicked at the door.

"Can't she start a fire that way?" asked Naomi.

"That's what she's trying to do," he said. "Is Kenny still in there?"

"Oh Phil, I'm so sorry, but I didn't have any warning."

"Not your fault, Naomi. Would you run call an officer as fast as you can?"

She nodded, bit her lip, and scurried away.

Phil didn't think Maya could start a fire; these ship receptacles didn't operate the way the usual apartment units did, as self-contained high-temperature elements. He'd heard somewhere that on a spaceship the chutes were all connected centrally, for safety. He hoped he was right.

But he couldn't be sure of anything. He hurled himself against the door, trying to tear it from its hinges. Inside he could hear the baby wailing.

Holder knew that room, the one full of people staring at him. That was the top deck, the gallery where he'd caught Maya with that guy, whoever he was, had that big fight with her. Just before she went downstairs.

He hadn't seen them in there. But if Phil was with her, and if a guard was with them both . . .

Webbed polysteel struts passed in front of his face—the loading jetty. Suddenly he was dangling above a floodlit landing deck. Two suited crew members grabbed him by the arm, one on each side, and guided him toward an airlock. One reached up and unsnapped the curb by which he'd attached his suit harness to the lifeline. Holder sagged to his feet, exhausted.

They helped him into the airlock and tossed aside their own safety lines. The heavy doors slid together, interlocked, and sealed. A rush of sound, low at first, then louder, announced the return of atmospheric pressure. Red lights over the inner doors blinked to green. The two crew members kept their firm grip on him.

The inner doors slid aside. A brace of guards leveled fireguns at him; behind them it was too dark to see anything. "Take your suit off," said the man beside him, in a loud, hollow voice. "In here."

Holder stripped off his pressure suit. The two crew members stood back, watching, staying inside the lock with him and keeping their own suits on. He realized that if he tried anything they didn't like, they would simply close the lock again and evacuate it. He didn't blame them for being scared; he was scared too.

"We've recovered the unfortunate gentleman in excellent condition." One could almost hear the warm smile in the captain's mellow voice as it flowed from the speakers. "As promised, our own course and schedule have been completely unaffected."

The party guests broke into sympathetic applause. Richard Ruiz turned to Clarissa Sirich. "Quite an engaging performance, See. The captain neglected to tell us the name of the star."

She looked distracted. "Richard, your instinct for danger—is it well developed?"

"In politics?" Ruiz smiled delicately. "I assure you . . ."

"Immediate physical danger. I've got a strong sense for this kind of thing. Something's about to happen, something bad."

"Something just *did*, See. If that fellow had been a few seconds later . . . You're probably feeling the reaction."

She shrugged. "Maybe you're right." She sipped at her drink. "Tell me about your program."

He looked at her in surprise. "I've been talking about it for days!"

"Tell me again. While we walk." She hooked her finger in his jacket and tugged. He followed.

His eyes lit up. She really was an attractive woman, after all. He'd had little time for women since the death of his wife many years ago—not from lack of interest, but rather from lack of confidence, if the truth be told. Certainly he'd had no indication from Sirich that she thought of him in that way. The sense of danger, maybe? He'd always been impressed by those stories of fruit trees that blossomed frantically after they were cut down . . . He helped her push through the thinning crowd.

The captain's voice returned on the address system. "Despite all the excitement, our program has been moving along uninterrupted, as I've emphasized. And so, in just about five seconds now, we'll be lighting the annihilator. I'm sorry I won't be there with you in person for the traditional toasts, but things *have* been a little busy. Here we go . . ."

Another little cheer was punctuated by tipsy shrieks and laughter as the floor dropped away and then came right back up again a hair more vigorously than expected, like an elevator bumping to a rough stop. Three people fell down, whooping and giggling; still, the old hands in the crowd pronounced it a remarkably smooth cross-over.

"That's about as cleverly as we can do it," the captain was saying, but the rest of his remarks went unheard, for a woman ran screaming down the spiral stair from the gallery above.

"She's killed her! Call for help! Oh God, she's killed the guard!"

When Holder was stripped to the plain dark trousers and sweater he'd worn for the last several weeks aboard *Cormorant,* they gestured him into the interior and frisked him with a squealer. The airlock closed behind him. They led him up a flight of steps and through twisting corridors, under close escort all the way, and finally onto the darkened bridge.

The captain turned as Holder was brought to him. "You, sir, are the luckiest man I've ever met," he said.

"I hope to be luckier still, Captain. Where is Mrs. Holder now?"

"I've assigned two guards to be with her and her husband. If I may say so, sir, my staff has done things on your behalf that . . ."

"And I sincerely thank them for it, and I thank you, Captain. Would it be possible . . .?"

Ruby lights were suddenly flashing everywhere on the inter-communications board.

"Excuse me a moment," said the captain.

The security officer bent over the intercom, pressing phones to his ears, mumbling into the mike at his throat. Holder caught the words: ". . . damage control fire team to G, Room G-412. Assign one armed guard. Guard detachment to A, Room A-3 view gallery, seek armed woman dressed in white, extremely dangerous . . ."

Holder stared about wildly. The bridge personnel were distracted by the multiple outbreaks of bad news. He bolted for the open elevator door.

Behind him he heard the captain cry out, "Stop him! Stop that man!"

Angelica Claymore had memorized the layout of the ship as well as she could in the few days she'd been on board, but she hadn't had time to penetrate the maze of the command-and-control module. Rather than take a chance on losing herself among the winding corridors and catwalks and stair-wells that branched from the hangar deck, she preferred to take an elevator to the top. Take it by storm, if necessary.

Claymore heard running footsteps behind her. She wheeled around, leveled the firegun she'd lifted from the stunned guard, held steady a moment and then squeezed the trigger. Fire burst from the corridor wall. The first guard ran into the flames, then staggered away, shielding his eyes, dropping his weapon. There were screams and curses behind him, and for a moment no one else ventured beyond the protecting wall.

She heard the elevator whine beside her, stop, hiss open. She wheeled again, raised the gun a second time.

Holder himself!—bearded and stained with sweat, he cursed and pounded the lift controls, not sparing her so much as a glance.

She faltered, but wasted no time. She lifted the gun toward Holder's eyes; as soon as the moving barrel found its target, she would squeeze the trigger.

Squeeze it she did. But just before she did she felt her cheeks sag and her mouth suck and pop open involuntarily, and heavy eyelids come halfway down over her eyes. Her knees buckled, and when the gun went off it wasn't pointing at Holder at all, and the capsula burrowed under the wool carpet and discharged against the deck. A sluggish pool of fire erupted at her feet, and she didn't know if she had the strength to keep from falling into it.

The elevator, its safeties overridden by acceleration it was never designed to withstand, had already plummeted from her sight.

Holder was floating when the elevator stopped and the doors slid open, and he caromed off the ceiling, scrabbling to get a purchase on the doors before they closed. He pulled himself out into the hall just in time to be thrown savagely to the floor. He lay stunned and gasping.

Was he already too late? Reason screamed "yes" and told him to get to the lifeboats. If Maya had caused the disaster, then the damage was already done. But he couldn't give up now; he couldn't admit that salvation had slipped through his grasp a second time.

An old woman's body was lying on the floor a couple of meters away. Painfully her head lifted, and she turned her face toward him. *"I wondered if you would make it this far," said Clarissa Sirich,* forcing the words through her ancient sagging throat. "I must tell you . . ."

Holder had no time for lectures. Vividly he recalled the last moments of *Griffin*, the spasms of the disintegrating vessel. Only seconds remained. He pulled himself erect with agonizing effort and staggered past the prostrate body of Sirich—not even hearing the words she so desperately pushed into the air, he reeled in mock drunkenness toward that cabin, half a corridor away.

The weight lifted and everything felt normal. Holder knew it would not last, but he took what advantage he could, sprinting down the curving corridor. Around him sirens wailed and emergency lights flashed and the insistent voice of the address system ordered everyone to the hangar deck.

He found Phil lying groggily on the floor. Holder knew he'd been thrown against the far wall and wouldn't recover for another minute. By then . . .

He faced the door. At forty-three Holder was fatter and shorter of breath, but he was also stronger, more determined, and cared less about pain. He kicked at the door with all his power. To his astonishment, it flew in without resistance.

He stepped forward. Heat and light expanded from the

recycler aperture at the far end of the little cabin. Holder got his hands in front of his eyes just before he was bathed in flame. The force of expanding gases slapped the door shut in his face, saving his life; he was left with the sharp stench of burned hair and cloth.

He grabbed at the twisted door handle, screaming in agony at its fiery touch. The door was already melting as he pushed it open against the howling inferno inside.

He hardly felt the hands on his shoulders, pulling him away, and in the strength of his rage he could easily have resisted them if the dying ship had not convulsed again, throwing him to the floor along with his would-be rescuers. He found himself smashed into the carpet, felt its rough weave pressing into his flesh. He was staring into Phil's crushed, horror-stricken face only centimeters away. "Listen," Holder said, forcing his lips of putty to form the words. "You'll survive. You'll live to come back, as I did. What you have to do is . . ."

Then they were hurled, weightless, against the ceiling. He was tumbling in the smoke-fouled air, and Phil was lost, and there was old Sirich floating in front of him. "Why didn't you listen to me?" she shouted. "Time . . ."

He ignored her again. "Phil, where are you, man? I've got to tell you—"

Sirich cut through in the sharpest tones he'd ever heard from her. "Let him go! You can not improve his life, Holder, you can only shorten it."

"Phil! For my sake—"

"You'll kill him for your sake! He must get to the hangar deck with the others, don't you *remember?*"

Flames poured into the corridor. from cabins on both sides whose doors had melted away. Fire roiled crazily around them and below them in the turbulent currents of weightless air. Reflexively Holder retreated. "Phil!"

A faint shout came from up ahead. "This way, T.T."

Holder started to swim faster through the smoke, but Sirich's hand on his shoulder kept him back easily. "Will you let go? Will you accept your life—his life—and live it? Or will you condemn yourself to this eternity of failure?"

He looked at her aged face, and then down at his blistered and charred hands. He stared at her out of red eyes set in a face bearded with ash. He began to weep.

Through the flames Angelica Claymore watched black and red silhouettes of passengers being efficiently herded along the hangar deck toward assigned life capsules and launches. She admired the expertise of the ship's personnel as they kept their groups organized, rounding them up when zero-gee episodes threatened to scatter them, helping them to keep going when explosive accelerations slapped them to their knees. Claymore admired the ship's personnel, but she had her own job to do—twice she'd discouraged crew members who'd looked as if they were thinking of requisitioning the Sprint.

She sat with her back to the open airlock door, an oxygen mask clamped to her face. Her white silks were blackened and torn. Her internal monologue was a string of expletives—she badly wanted to get aboard the Sprint and tell it to get her out of here.

But Sirich had said she'd be waiting in the Sprint, and—damn the old woman!—she wasn't.

Claymore was highly intelligent, but as an activist she liked to deal in simple emotions. She wasn't going to worry about whether Sirich was using her again. In spite of everything she still *liked* Sirich, and she would guard the ship until the old woman showed up, or until she herself was forced to flee.

With a start Claymore recognized Ted Macklin in the flickering shadows on the far side of the hangar deck—Theodore Macklin, soon to be Speaker of the United States of North America and self-proclaimed "hero" of the wreck of the *Griffin*—trying to push his way to the head of a line of weeping socialites, only to be forcibly restrained by a young officer and made to wait his turn.

How easy it would have been in that moment to add one single well-aimed firebolt to the inferno of smoke and flames, to incinerate the panic-stricken Macklin in his tracks! In an instant Claymore would have reversed her mission's purpose at its causal root.

Concurrently with that shocking temptation came an even more astounding thought—that it wouldn't make any difference! That Sirich was right, Claymore's proper past would forever be her proper past and could not be changed either in memory or reality. And something more as well, that without Macklin Earth would follow the path to its self-determined perdition anyway, unless she were willing to shoulder the intolerable burden of returning again and again to adjust each human error. How many Doppels would she lose on each fix-it trip? How many universes would eventually benefit from her efforts? Was she willing to play the goddess, as Sirich had suggested?

These jarring ideas formed and dissipated in far less time than she would have needed to express them aloud, and by the time she had disciplined her rebellious spirit, Ted Macklin had disappeared from her view.

Finally Sirich, that nimble crone, appeared running lightly across the webbed steel flooring, holding a mask to her face. Behind her came Holder.

At the sight of Holder the firegun twitched reflexively in Claymore's hand; with him, she had to make a positive effort to counteract her self-induced conditioning. All around her the disintegrating ship gave evidence that her mission was complete, that Holder had been too late.

Another lurch, and a chattering vibration ran through the ship, and the very walls began to howl. Claymore knew the end must be at hand.

They were weightless again, and Sirich and Holder were floundering. Sirich was the luckier—her last step had aimed her precisely at the airlock, and she flew right into it. Claymore, keeping a grip on the frame of the lock, threw away the firegun and stretched out her hand to catch Philip Holder.

Perhaps it would be useful, she thought, to clean up all the extratemporal debris.

Her fingers closed on his bloody, stiffened hand.

36

Once on a hot summer day Holder had been sitting on a balcony on Parnassus, sipping a glass of wine, when he became aware of a constant popping sound almost at the threshold of his hearing. The first thing he noticed when he started looking for the source of the sound was that his table had been sprinkled with fine seeds, like carroway on a bun. He swept them away, and within a minute or two more had appeared. Then he realized that the popping sound came from the adjacent hedge, a bush with densely packed, small, hard, shiny leaves, each branch ending in a stalk of dozens of clustered seed pods. Under the influence of the summer sun the pods were exploding, launching the seeds blindly outward. He wondered what fraction of this prodigal spray of life would survive.

The Sprint stood off a few hundred kilometers as *Griffin* broke apart. Life capsules and launches fled the stricken liner with little thought for their final destination. Only a tiny proportion of the ship's solidified superhydrogen elements had mingled—producing a series of powerful explosions that dispersed the remainder—but the space around the ship coruscated with random interactions, spewing energetic particles in all directions.

Yellow radiation warnings glowed on the Sprint's boards. The ship's occupants were bundled into thick radiation suits; Holder's, originally intended for the portly Unwin, was much too large.

"There it goes," said Claymore. The screens guttered with an oily mass of flame, darkened almost to blackness by electronic filter circuits, but too bright to be suppressed entirely. Like a film of a falling rock shown upside down at twice the normal rate, the wreck of the *Griffin* fell straight up into the void.

"Two-plus gees for almost an entire day," said Sirich. "You're there, Philip. So is Macklin. He didn't make it to a life capsule, lucky for him, though he probably climbed over a few children trying."

The viewscreens gradually irised open as the offending radiation diminished, until the stars grew bright, filling the darkness like a mass of spilled diamonds glistening with cold, eternal light.

"The neighborhood's cooled off," said Claymore. "Let's get out of these." She unstrapped herself, floated out of her couch, and began pulling her suit apart.

Holder spoke for the first time since he'd been dragged aboard. "They weren't in the cabin," he said in a voice dry as dead coals. "Maya and Kenny. They weren't in there."

"I was trying to tell you that," Sirich said, ripping open her suit.

Claymore plucked the hood from the unmoving Holder's head and started helping him with the fastenings of his suit.

He blinked naked eyelids at Sirich. "When did you know? A year ago? Twenty years ago?"

"Let's say I knew with certainty about twenty minutes ago," she said, folding the suit and stowing it in the locker with Claymore's. "When I saw the woman from across the corridor carry your baby toward the elevators, before you arrived."

"Naomi," he said. He paused. "But you were already waiting for me."

Claymore briskly but carefully pulled his gloves off for him; his hands were cracked and bloody. She carried the gloves to the cleaning receptacle, fastidiously, with her fingertips.

"We should get you started on burn treatments right away, Philip," said Sirich. "You'll have nasty scars."

He shook his head. "I'm thirsty," he said; then, "I want to hear the rest."

Claymore impatiently pulled a water bottle from a wall panel and held it for him as he sucked eagerly. "You'll have to take care of yourself after this, Holder. I'm not your nurse."

He kept sucking, and then pulled his mouth away. "Okay," he said. "I'll take care of myself. But I want to hear."

"I want to hear too, Clarissa," Claymore said as she replaced the bottle.

"All the worlds you sought to preserve are still intact, Angelica. Your efforts to make things come out the way they are going to come out anyway are quite as touching as Philip's efforts to change them." Sirich looked at Holder. "Surely you understand by now that your wife had nothing to do with the wreck of the *Griffin,* Philip? And that you could not have prevented it in any case."

"The fire—"

"When I was a little girl on Earth my father told me of a great electrical power failure he had experienced as a young man. Many cities in what was then the United States were affected, including New York. What sticks in my mind was his story of the little boy who had been playing with a bread toaster, against his mother's strict orders, and who plugged in the forbidden machine at the precise moment when the lights went out—everywhere. The little boy would never believe he was not personally responsible."

Claymore looked at Sirich quizzically. "When did this happen, exactly?"

"Oh, before your time." Sirich bent forward from her seat and took Holder's hands in her own, inspecting them gently. "The fire that came from the recycler was not set by Maya's naive efforts, Philip," she said. She gave him a wan smile. "I'm sure the machine was happily gobbling everything she was feeding it, notably the contents of your suitcase. The recyclers were centrally connected to a fusion torch. Backflash from an explosion in the annihilator must have come through all of them at once."

"And Maya?"

Sirich released his hands and leaned back. "I've studied the records of the aftermath more carefully than either of you. There is no mention of anyone who could have been her, either among the survivors or the known dead. In that respect her fate is no different from half the others aboard."

An involuntary gasp escaped Holder's lips. Claymore looked at his ashen face: fine beads of perspiration stood out on his forehead. "I'm putting you in the infirmary, Holder, before you go into deep shock."

Sirich helped Claymore unbuckle him, and roll him out of his suit and the rest of his clothes. He did not protest, but he repeated Kenny's name.

"His name isn't Kenny now, Philip," said Sirich as she worked. "And in my proper time he is as old as you are. You see, I had a premonition of danger—even in the absence of the spectacular show you put on for us this time around, Philip—and I managed to be on one of the first launches to get away. Just before they sealed us in, a crewman brought a baby on with him. He said he'd found him in a dead woman's arms. I didn't know who he was; now I do."

"He's alive—I could—"

"I'll tell you this much: he is healthy; he is more or less content. You have no right to hope for more. No human has the right to hope for anything more, for any other. Later I'll let you decide if you really need the details."

They finished stripping Holder naked, and then carefully arranged him inside the Sprint's infirmary berth. The Sprint was as well equipped medically as it was militarily; one kind of preparedness implied the other.

"You can be as ruthless as any goddess, but you're not ominscient. Unwin has betrayed you, as you had hoped—and he's betrayed me too, though I will manage, by sheer good luck and quick thinking, to survive that bit of trickery on my own. I never did like that man.

"I write in the confidence (which you gave me) that causality can not be violated, because it does not exist across the boundaries of the universes, only within them. You claim there are no loops in space-time, only spirals. Well, you're the theorist, not me. But thermodynamics works always and everywhere, and I'm not above trying to insure that things come out all right for the me who just left here, as well as they did for me who got back here a couple of years ago and has been hiding out in that absurd think tank. I wouldn't mind seeing you make things hot for that S.O.B. Unwin, as long as you don't do anything drastic.

"I know I'm cheating, telling you I'm back and alive—you were always so careful not to spoil the fun for your selves and other friends. I, on the other hand, have always been something of a spoiler. This far I'll tantalize you—I'll tell you I got almost everything a human has a right to hope for. Thanks to you.

"I love you, you thousand-year-old hag."

(unsigned)

Holder punched the send key of the public terminal, then walked along the inner balcony of the soleri toward the familiar apartment door.

Susan heard the buzzer. "Who is it?" she said. The screen showed only the balcony outside, people passing to and fro in silence.

"You'll recognize my voice," said the speaker. "Don't use my name."

She did recognize the voice, but she didn't believe it. She pushed the key that let whoever was out there see her face. "Is that really you?" she said suspiciously. "How can you be *here*, Ph—"

"Please!" he said. "I'm not that man." He stepped into the camera's view. He looked made-over, as if he were just back from a long vacation—or a short stay in the hospital. "I'm not the man you think I am."

She stared at him for a long time. "You couldn't be, could you? We heard you disappeared two days ago. You would have had to get back here almost as fast as light. And that's impossible."

"I'm glad you understand." He paused. "Are you afraid of me?"

She nodded. She looked away from the screen. She felt cold, and hugged herself.

"Will you meet me someplace? In public? How about Alejandro's, say in five minutes—I'll buy you a drink."

"He drank," she said.

"I don't. Not like that."

She thought about it, but she'd known he would ask, and she'd known her answer, as soon as she saw his face. "I'm a curious fool, but okay. What should I call you?"

"I'm with the FRAME Corporation. My name is—now don't laugh—"

But she laughed anyway.

Many nights later she moved against him in the darkness of her room. "I believe you now. You're not the same man at all."

But Holder was not ready for sleep; he kept talking even as they lowered the cabinet's transparent lid. "You could have told me, Clarissa. You already knew . . ."

"Hush. You would not have believed what I could have told you, and I did not yet know what *you* wanted to know. Sleep now. We'll talk again when you get up."

The lid closed on Holder. Claymore pressed a sequence of keys on the side of the cabinet, waiting until she saw a pattern of lights that satisfied her. The lid grew opaque and Holder disappeared.

Claymore found Sirich in the cabin, changing into fresh work clothes. It was uncharacteristic of her to undress so openly; Claymore noted with interest the firm smooth muscles under the wrinkled skin. "So, Clarissa, you were experimenting with him as well as with me?"

Sirich looked at her with surprise. "I was never experimenting with you, Angelica—you were the means of the experiment, not the subject of it." She zipped up her coveralls. "I planted enough hints to scare Mr. Speaker Theodore Macklin into sending someone after Holder when he jumped the *Humboldt*, and I knew exactly how to do it; though I didn't know that the someone he sent would be you. You are an accident, Angelica, but I rather like you. In that respect, you are to me what a daughter might have been."

"How should I take that?" Claymore asked coolly, as she began to change her own clothes.

"Take it this way." Sirich reached out to the young woman, took her by the shoulder, kissed her on the cheek. For an instant she held her close, then let go. "I like you, despite the words I used when I was trying to free you from yourself. If I weren't such a cynic, I might say I've grown to love you."

Claymore looked away, her throat tense. "How do I know, this time . . ."

"I was telling the truth that time, too. I like you anyway."

Angelica Claymore yanked her jacket closed and settled into the pilot's seat, drawing the straps across her chest like armor. The boards displayed the Sprint's status—fueled, provisioned, sealed, ready for any assignment. "What now, old woman?" she said gruffly.

Sirich laughed. "You can't insult me with the facts, daughter." She slipped into the right-hand seat and buckled herself in. "The choice is yours: all of time is opened before you. Past and present are one, of course, minor variations on a theme—you've seen that for yourself. Would you like to go straight home to Earth? There you're a girl of, what, ten years?"

Claymore did not reply immediately. "If I could, I would change things," she said at last. "Like Holder wanted to. But it can't be done—that was your experiment, wasn't it? That's what you proved."

"It's true I helped him make a determined assault on history. Let's say the outcome supported the predictions of theory. If you want to throw your life on the roulette wheel, there's room for a small change or two. . . ."

"Not enough. Small changes are not enough." Claymore studied the instruments, feeling with her mind for the patterns of potential they encoded. "What about the future?"

"The future!" Sirich laughed with scorn. "Certainly, nothing is easier! But you'll find the future very dull in this neighborhood." Sirich looked at the starry skies pictured in the viewscreens: unseen in those wide-angle views were the fleeing life boats—those that would disappear forever, those that would survive to reappear in some distant place and time. Sirich resumed talking; she was subdued. "We were early away. In our eagerness to escape we depleted our fuel supply, and at a crucial moment our engines failed. We brushed the holes, and emerged a thousand years into the future—"

"A thousand years!"

"And Darwin had not changed! In a thousand years not one man or woman of vision will arise to grasp the essential nature of what I sought to do there. I wanted to understand the nature of transformation; *they* were content—all of them, for a thousand years!—to celebrate the past. Tame dinosaurs!" She looked at Claymore then, and Claymore saw that the old woman's eyes were bright. "They wrote books about me!" said Sirich. "They made *statues* of me! But they knew less of me than you do."

Claymore looked away, unable to bear the woman's intense, demanding gaze. "Perhaps we should let Holder vote," she said. "After all, it's for his sake that we're here."

"I already know his vote," Sirich said. "Would you like me to tell it to you?"

I watched you emerge from your cocoon, the palms of your hands fresh and pink, your skin all clear and brown as a baby's, and I thought to myself, "Here is a new man come forth into the world, purged and cleansed by the fires of experience, ready to live . . ."

Of course I should have known you better.

"You used *me," you said. Those were your first words.*

Oh Philip, I wanted to cry, I wanted to laugh, I wanted to hit you! But I explained things to you instead.

I told you of my work in Special Projects, so far behind me now in my proper time—that after a century of study and experiment I was on the edge of describing mathematical parameters for the evolutionary potential of the human organism. I had calculated theoretical limits to what could be learned from detailed analyses of the structure and function of the brain, I had estimated the boundaries of ignorance inherent in statistical treatments of social behavior—utility matrices, game theories, and so on—and I had at last accepted the essential poverty of that behavioral pseudo-genetics once so quaintly known as "sociobiology." You might say I was trying to get the animal nature of people to precipitate out in a lump of numbers; the volatile stuff that remained would, I hoped, be refined humanity.

Then the wreck of the Griffin *intervened, and I was confronted with the futility of my efforts. A thousand years had passed; the human race had caught the social and spiritual paralysis of functional immortality. I'd tried to isolate it, in myself—they thanked me for failing.*

Biology lost its charms (I saw nothing left in the science but to amuse oneself creating monsters), so I drifted off into the cold and—as I thought—impractical realms of cosmology. There, to my surprise, I found new hope.

Remember, Philip, how we spoke of the world as an infinitely deep ocean, layered with thin horizontal currents flowing this way and that? And how the little sea creatures that live in these universe-currents go jostling through their lives unaware of their infinite one-to-one counterparts, all of whom are doing exactly the same thing at the same time? You were the bold little diatom (you and all your Doppels*) who submerged himself and lingered a while in a backward flowing current, to re-emerge in your counterpart's universe before he had left it . . .*

Well, I was bold before you, Philip, and I shall go on being bold long after your thin shell of lime has dissolved. I and all my Doppelgängers *are stones falling into the deep. Each eternity is a moment to me, and my only hope of change lies in sampling as many alternative forevers as I can. So I will go as far down into the infinite ocean of universes as I can, in the only direction I can, until every last version of me has been crushed out of existence by the pressure of change.*

Space is a resonant cavity of possibilities, Philip, and the universes are standing waves, phasing, reinforcing, abrading each other into identity—but there is leakage; way out there near the edges there is change.

In measuring myself against survivable change I hope to grasp again the nature of human nature. Yes, I used you in this experiment, but I helped you too; when I came back from the thousand-year reign to my ur-home on Earth I found a man determined to remake his life. I gave you certain tools, and with them you have helped me test my still crude and tentative model; you have given me both negative and positive evidence to work with.

You have confirmed that curiosity is needed; and tolerance for incomplete or ambiguous answers (the stumbling block of all religions); coupled with persistence, and determination to discover the truth. But equally necessary—and here you excel—is an obsession for doing things until you either get them right or something new pops out.

What I have described are the conditions of creation. The determination to create is the essence of humanity, and it now appears that to preserve humanity it will be necessary to circumvent the dead, deterministic hand of the cosmos itself. On some scale, perhaps, that has always been true.

Well, your would-be assassin and I have decided to join forces and go off universe-hunting. We're dropping you off where you said you'd like to go; perhaps one of these days we'll pop back in and check up on your progress . . .

Re-entry: Earth, 206 N.E.

Experience remains, of course, the sole criterion of the physical utility of a mathematical construction. But the creative principle resides in mathematics. In a certain sense, therefore, I hold it true that pure thought can grasp reality, as the ancients dreamed.
—Albert Einstein, *On the method of theoretical physics*